DINOSAURS

DESTROY

DETROIT

Johnathan Rand's 'Michigan Chillers':

#1: Mayhem on Mackinac Island

#2: Terror Stalks Traverse City

#3: Poltergeists of Petoskey

#4: Aliens Attack Alpena

#5: Gargoyles of Gaylord

#6: Strange Spirits of St. Ignace

#7: Kreepy Klowns of Kalamazoo

#8: Dinosaurs Destroy Detroit

#9: Sinister Spiders of Saginaw

#10 Mackinaw City Mummies

American Chillers:

#1: The Michigan Mega-Monsters

and more coming soon!

AudioCraft Publishing, Inc.
PO Box 281
Topinabee Island, MI 49791

#8: Dinosaurs Destroy Detroit

Johnathan
Rand

An AudioCraft Publishing, Inc. book

Graphics layout/design consultant: Chuck Beard, Straits Area Printing

The publisher gratefully acknowledges services provided by Travis & Renee Conners and *Rental Express*, Indian River, Michigan. (231) 238-9696

ISBN 1-893699-14-5

Printed in USA

Third Printing, November 2001

Dinosaurs Destroy Detroit

Visit the official 'Chillers' web site at:

www.americanchillers.com

Featuring excerpts from upcoming stories, interviews, and helpful hints for young writers! PLUS-find out how to join the official

'AMERICAN CHILLERS' FAN CLUB!

1

I've always thought it would be great to travel through time. To go back and see what happened during some particular era, or even go into the future to see what it would be like a thousand years from now. I know it's not possible, but it sure would be cool.

But when my grandpa said that once, every fifty years, you could do just that—using a window through time—I didn't believe him. I thought he was just telling me a story.

Grandpa said that once, every fifty years, on June 28th, at exactly 3:05 in the afternoon, a window through time would open up. A window that would allow a person to step through and travel in time, but only for a period of seven days. He said that the window was in a field not far from where I lived. His father had told him about it, and his father before him. That's how he knew about it.

Yeah, right. Like I was going to believe *that.*

But on June 28th of this year, at exactly 3:05 in the afternoon, I found out that my grandpa hadn't been trying to fool me. Because my friend Summer and I found the window through time . . . and what followed set off a chain of events that the city of Detroit wouldn't soon forget.

On the morning of Monday, June 28th, I was awakened by the lawnmower outside. Dad was working in the yard, and so was Mom. Dad works overnight at the factory, so he gets home at about eight in the morning and usually goes to work in the yard for a while before he goes to bed. Once a week he mows the lawn, and this was one of those mornings. When that mower fires up, it's no use trying to sleep anymore. It sounds like the space shuttle taking off!

But I suddenly remembered something: today was Monday.

Not just any Monday.

It was Monday, the 28th of June. This was the day Grandpa said that the window through time would open.

That is, of course, if there even was such a thing — and if I could find it.

I got dressed and sat down in the kitchen for a quick breakfast. The phone rang while I was eating a bowl of *Froot Loops*.

"Hello?" I answered, picking up the receiver.

"Nick? It's Summer. Are we still going today?"

Summer McCready is one of my best friends. She was one of the first people I met when I moved to Detroit, and she's pretty cool. We go to the same school and ride the same bus. Yesterday, I told her about the window through time. She didn't laugh like I thought she would.

In fact, she was fascinated.

"Let's go find it!" she'd said excitedly. I told

her to call me in the morning, and we'd make plans.

"You bet we're still going!" I replied, chomping on my cereal. "Otherwise, we won't have another chance for fifty years."

"Do you really think it's true?" she asked.

"I don't know," I pondered. "I asked my dad, and he just laughed. He said that Grandpa had told him about the window, but he didn't believe it. He never went to look for it."

My excitement was growing by the second, but so was my fear.

What if we really found the window? Would we travel back in time? Would we travel forward? That would be cool!

Either way, I was more than willing to spend an afternoon trying to find the window through time.

We agreed to meet at one o'clock at a corner store that wasn't far from my house. From there, we would ride our bikes to find the field that Grandpa talked about.

I got to the store just before one, and went inside. I bought a coke for each of us, along with a couple *Slim Jims*, and a camera. One of those disposable ones that they sell for a few dollars. If there really was such a thing as a 'window through time' I wanted to have pictures of what we saw.

Summer showed up right on time, as usual, and we biked for miles . . . through neighborhoods, down strange streets, past tall buildings. I know my grandpa said the field wasn't far from where I lived, but man . . . I think we biked ten miles!

Just before three o'clock, we found the field that my grandpa was talking about.

It was just like he'd said. The field was strewn with large rocks and old junk that had been placed there long ago. The rusted-out shell of an old car sat alone like a huge steel skeleton. Insects buzzed in the afternoon heat, and a chipmunk darted in front of us, chattering angrily at our presence.

On the south end of the field stood a large clump of trees. The trees were big . . . much bigger than Grandpa had described them. But I guess you'd expect them to be, since Grandpa hadn't seen them in fifty years.

That was where the window through time was supposed to open up. Within the stand of trees at the south end of the field.

There was too much debris strewn through the field to ride our bikes, so we walked, pushing them alongside. We drank the cokes and ate the *Slim Jims* as we walked.

When we reached the shade of the trees, we stopped. Summer's long blonde hair swept gently in the light afternoon breeze.

"What are we supposed to be looking for?" she asked, her eyes searching the field.

"I'm not really sure," I replied. "My grandpa said that it was just a big—"

Had I been able to finish my sentence, I would have said the words 'shimmering window'.

But I didn't get the chance to finish what I was saying . . . because right before us, at exactly 3:05, a thundering roar tore through the sky. It was the screeching sound of metal on metal, and it was *loud*.

Summer cupped her hands over her ears, and I did the same. I was shocked by the sudden noise—but it was nothing compared to the shock I received when I saw what was happening in the air right before my eyes.

2

Right before us, the window appeared! It opened like a nightshade, sweeping down toward the ground. It was about twenty feet wide and very high . . . taller than a house! It was as if a fuzzy gray sheet had been placed in the air right in front of us.

Then the grayness began to fade, giving way to a shimmering, clear window. I could see right through it! However, objects on the other side of the window—tree trunks, leaves, branches—they seemed to sway and bend. It was like looking at something through wavering heat waves.

I couldn't speak. My mouth was open, but I didn't know what to say. The noise had stopped, and all we could hear were a few birds chirping, and the sounds of the city in the distance.

The sun beamed down, and a trickle of sweat dripped down my forehead. I reached up and swept it away.

"Oh my gosh," Summer whispered. *"It's here! It's really here!"*

The window shimmered in front of us.

Did we dare? Should we step through?

I could think of a million reasons why we shouldn't.

But I could think of a *billion* reasons why we *should!*

"You wanna do this?" I asked hesitantly.

Summer turned her head and looked at me. "What do you think?" she asked. Her voice was soft, and maybe a bit fearful. Now that we had discovered that my grandpa was right—that there really *was* a window—we weren't too sure about the whole idea of time travel.

"Let's try," I urged, nodding my head. "You

hold onto my hand, and I'll step through. If there's a problem, you can pull me back. Simple."

Summer looked at the shimmering window, then turned and looked at me.

"Okay," she agreed. "Let's try it."

I took a step toward the window, and Summer followed. She held her hand out, and I took it in mine.

"If I squeeze your hand really hard, pull me back," I instructed. She nodded, understanding.

"Good luck, Nick," she said.

I turned and faced the strange, wavering window, took a deep breath . . . and stepped through.

3

I'm not sure what I expected, but I'll tell you what: there was *nothing* I could have imagined that would have prepared me for what I saw.

I found myself in a jungle! The air was thick and humid, and the sky was overcast and gray. Enormous ferns grew close by, and giant trees with wide, thick leaves towered above me. I could hear a creek babbling not far off.

And a volcano! Miles away, I could see a

smoking volcano, spewing out ash and black smoke into the sky.

Where had I traveled to? Had I traveled back in time . . . or forward?

In two seconds, I had my answer, and it came from out of the sky. I heard a loud screech, and suddenly a gigantic bird appeared! It was far bigger than any other bird I had ever seen before. It looked like a small plane coasting over the treetops.

Wait a minute! I thought. *That's not a bird at all! That's . . . that's a flying reptile! It's a Quetzalcoatlus! I know it is!*

A Quetzalcoatlus is a winged reptile that lived during the Cretaceous period, about 65 million years ago. They're huge, with wing-spans of nearly forty feet! It's the largest flying animal ever discovered. I learned all about them when we studied dinosaurs in science class.

The giant, winged beast flew overhead, finally disappearing into the thick trees.

Wow! I had traveled back in time 65 million years! Back to the land of dinosaurs!

I was still holding Summer's hand. When I turned to see her, I got a surprise.

The window looked the same on this side as it

did on the other! I could see trees and ferns on the other side, but they seemed to waver back and forth. Summer was nowhere to be found.

I looked at my hand, but —

It was *gone!* It had vanished just above my wrist!

Where my hand met the window, it disappeared — like I had dipped my hand into a pool of gray water!

But I could still feel Summer's tight grasp. She was holding on firmly, just like I'd asked her to do.

She had to see this. I pulled, wanting her to come through the fuzzy, shimmering window.

I could feel her resisting. I think that maybe she was trying to pull me back, but I wanted her to see what I was seeing. She just *had* to see this!

I pulled with all my might. Suddenly, she came tumbling through the window. I lost my balance and I fell, and she came crashing down on top of me.

"I thought you were in trouble!" she exclaimed, standing up and brushing herself off. "I thought that —"

When she noticed where she was, she stopped speaking, not finishing her sentence. Her mouth hung open like a dead fish, and her eyes swirled about as she took in the strange surroundings.

"It's . . . it's . . . ." she stammered. She was too stunned to speak.

"It's the age of dinosaurs!" I finished for her. "We traveled back in time, millions and millions of years!"

We stared for a long, long time. Neither of us moved. Strange, animal-like sounds came from the thick jungle. It was all too bizarre, too unreal to even believe. I have seen paintings and drawings of what scientists believe the dinosaur era was like, but this was just too far-out to even imagine.

"Come on," I said, taking a few steps toward a clump of ferns.

"Where are you going?" Summer asked, her voice filled with astonishment.

"I just want to go and check this place out a little more. Come on."

"What if we get lost?" she asked. "What then?"

She had a point. We couldn't wander too far from the window, or we might not be able to find our way back to it. Then, we'd never make it back through time. Dad would ground me for a month.

Wait a minute, I thought. *If we never made it back, how could Dad ground me?*

Either way, it wasn't a pleasant thought.

"We'll stay close by, I promise," I assured Summer. "Come on." I extended my hand, and she reluctantly began walking toward me.

"Okay," she reluctantly agreed. "But let's not go far."

As fate would have it, we wouldn't get very far at all. We hadn't taken more than ten steps when we heard a loud noise in front of us. It was the sound of crunching branches and limbs.

Summer and I ducked behind a thick stand of small trees. The noise grew louder, and the heavy snapping and crunching drew closer. We nestled into the leaves, hoping that we were hidden.

Suddenly, we saw it, and I gasped out loud.

A dinosaur!

It was only twenty feet from us — and it was HUGE!

But what was even stranger: I recognized the beast!

"*It's a Triceratops!*" I whispered to Summer. "*I've seen them in my dinosaur books!*"

"*Great,*" Summer replied. "*At least we know

what kind of dinosaur we're going to be eaten by!"

I shook my head. *"No,"* I assured her. *"The Triceratops is a plant-eater. They don't eat meat."*

"Let's hope so," Summer said.

Triceratops is a cool-looking dinosaur. They have three horns that protrude from their face, and a large, bony plate behind the back of the skull. One short horn is perched above the dinosaur's bird-like beak, and two longer horns stick out just above the creature's eyes. The dinosaur walks on four strong, thick, legs. Triceratops looks like a huge rhinoceros.

We watched the creature as it continued slowly on its path. It didn't pay any attention to us. It acted as though we weren't even there.

I quickly thrust my hand into my pocket, pulled out my disposable camera, and clicked off a couple pictures of the Triceratops.

Suddenly, the huge dinosaur stopped — and chewed on some leaves!

"See?" I whispered to Summer. *"Just plants. I don't think that he'll hurt us."*

I was right, of course. The Triceratops wouldn't hurt us.

What I didn't know was that there was a creature sneaking up behind us at that very moment that *could* hurt us.

And I was about to know the real meaning of fear — because we were about to come face-to-face with a Tyrannosaurus Rex.

4

The Triceratops was moving away when we heard a noise behind us. It was a long, deliberate crunch, like something heavy was advancing slowly through the brush.

Like it was stalking something.

I turned, and the sight behind me almost made me faint.

The beast that was towering above us was unmistakable. I'd seen drawings before, and I'd seen the movie *Jurassic Park*.

It was a Tyrannosaurus Rex.

I knew right then we were in deep trouble.

Summer turned, and when she saw the terrible beast looming over us, she screamed. I quickly grabbed her arm and told her to stop.

"No!" I hissed. *"Be quiet! Maybe the T-Rex can't see us!"*

But Summer was too frightened. She jumped up and did the worst possible thing she could do.

She ran.

"Summer!" I shouted. *"Stop! STOP!"*

But it was too late. She had already sprang from our hiding place.

Not knowing what else to do, and thinking that the huge dinosaur had probably spotted us by now, I jumped up and ran after her.

Behind me, the T-Rex let out a terrible, loud screech. Trees snapped like toothpicks as the horrendous beast began charging after us.

The problem was, he was attacking from behind us—cutting off our way back to the window through time! We were trapped!

"Nick!" Summer shouted from in front of me. "A cave! There's a small cave up ahead!"

I couldn't see the cave that she was talking about, so I had no choice but to follow her and hope she was right.

Suddenly, she fell to the ground and scrambled forward on her hands and knees.

She was right! At the bottom of the wall of solid rock was a small opening. In a flash, Summer was gone.

By now, the giant dinosaur was right behind me. The ground quaked with every thundering step it took.

I couldn't afford to waste any time. I leapt forward, landing on my elbows . . . but it was too late! The T-Rex attacked, and caught my foot in his mouth!

"Ahhhhhhh!!!!" I screamed at the top of my lungs. I was scrambling forward into the cave, trying desperately to pull my foot away from the terrible grip of the dinosaur. *"Aaaahhhhh!!!!!"*

In the darkness of the small cave, Summer grabbed my hands and pulled. I was in a dangerous tug-of-war between Summer—and a vicious, bloodthirsty dinosaur!

Suddenly, my shoe slipped off of my foot—and it saved my life! Only my shoe was taken—not my foot.

I jerked my leg into the cave, and just in time. I could see the T-Rex's huge jaws at the mouth of the cave, snapping and chewing, trying to get us.

And on top of that, his breath was awful!

After a few terrifying minutes, the dinosaur became frustrated. The noise outside the small cave stopped, and the ground shook as the beast stormed away to search for other forms of food. As the giant dinosaur thundered off, I leaned down, held out the camera, and snapped a picture.

"I can't believe that just happened!" Summer gasped. "We were attacked by a *real live* dinosaur!"

I knelt down, peering out the opening of the cave, making sure the dinosaur was gone. After a few minutes, I felt it was safe to leave the shelter of the cave.

"Come on," I said. "We've got to get back through the window. It's too dangerous to stay here."

We climbed out from beneath the rock ledge and stood up. Looking around, it was still hard to believe where we were.

"Nobody is going to believe us, Nick," Summer whispered. She turned her head, her eyes scanning the trees and sky.

"Yes, they will," I said confidently, holding out

my camera. "Here's the proof right here. Come on. Let's go back through the window."

Thankfully, we weren't far from the window through time. From where I stood, I could see the strange glistening window through the trees.

We crept cautiously toward it, wary of any dinosaurs that might be around.

We were almost to the window when Summer suddenly stopped in her tracks.

"Look!" she cried out, pointing toward some bushes. I stopped and turned, looking to see what she was pointing at.

Beneath a tree, in a clump of dried branches and leaves . . . was an *egg!* There was no mistaking it.

"It's a dinosaur egg!" I said excitedly. "It's a *real* dinosaur egg!"

I snapped my head around to make sure there weren't any dinosaurs nearby, then sprinted to the large, oval object.

It was an egg, all right. It was just a bit bigger than a bowling ball, and shaped almost like a chicken egg, only a bit rounder. It was a dirty gray color, with blacks specks all over it.

I knelt to the ground on one knee and touched the egg with my finger. It was smooth and warm.

Then I reached both hands around it, and picked it up.

"What are you going to do with that?" Summer asked, her voice filled with apprehension. I'm sure she already knew what I had in mind, and I don't think she liked the idea one bit.

"Just in case the pictures don't turn out," I said, "this will be our proof. We'll have a real dinosaur egg to show everyone. This will *prove* that we traveled back through time."

I could tell Summer didn't like the plan, but she didn't say anything more. Besides . . . I was going to return to the future with the dinosaur egg whether Summer liked it or not.

And that's how this whole mess got started. Two worlds were about to collide . . . bringing a panic and terror that the city of Detroit had never before known.

5

Getting back through the time window was easy enough. Getting the dinosaur egg home was difficult, but I managed.

Getting people to believe me was the problem.

I called my friend, Mike Parker. He just laughed. I called the Cranbrook Institute of Science and told them I had traveled back in time and had pictures of real dinosaurs, and they said I was a kook! They said that if I called them again, they were going to call the police!

The next day, I developed the pictures at one of those sixty-minute photo developing places at the department store. I kept my fingers crossed for the whole hour.

Please turn out, I thought. *Please turn out. Man, I hope the pictures turn out good.*

They did.

They were spectacular! The picture of the Triceratops was awesome! Even the picture of the T-Rex came out bright and clear!

I had it! I had proof! I couldn't wait to show my pictures to the world.

I pedaled my bike back to the newspaper offices. At the front desk, I showed my pictures to a woman who picked them up, looked at them, and handed them back to me, uninterested.

"Very good fakes," she smirked, walking away.

"Fakes?!?!?" I cried out. "What are you talking about?!?!? These are pictures of *real* dinosaurs! My friend Summer and I traveled back in time millions of years and—"

"Look," the woman interrupted sharply. "We don't have time for this. We are a very busy newspaper here. We report news that is true and real.

Not pictures that have obviously been doctored-up by a kid with a computer."

"Doctored-up!?!??!" I cried. "These pictures aren't doctored-up!"

"You kids can do anything with computers these days," the woman insisted. Her voice was tense, and I could tell she was growing impatient with me. "You probably took pictures of plastic toy dinosaurs and made them bigger in your computer," she presumed.

"But I have an egg!" I exclaimed. "I have a real dinosaur egg that I brought back. I can show it to you!"

"Well, in that case, just bring the egg in here," the woman replied. She picked up a piece of paper and began reading it to herself while she continued to speak to me. "Just bring in your little dinosaur egg and we'll have a look." She looked up from the paper, glaring at me. "By the way," she said with a wink, "you don't happen to have any pictures of the abominable snowman, too, do you?"

She was making fun of me!

Well, I was going to show her! I would simply go home, retrieve the dinosaur egg, and bring it back to the newspaper offices. Then she'd have to believe me!

I left the newspaper office without even saying good-bye. I pedaled my bike furiously home, whizzing past yards and down side streets.

I'll show her, I thought. *I'll show everyone. I've got a real dinosaur egg, and I'm going to prove it. Maybe Summer and I will even be on TV! We'll be heroes!*

I had placed the egg in a cardboard box and slid it beneath my bed. The last thing I wanted was my older sister to find it. Or anyone else, for that matter.

But when I walked into my house, I got the surprise of my life!

Our home was *ransacked!* A table was overturned, and a magazine rack had been knocked over! What on earth was going on?!?!? What had happened?!?!?

A sudden shuffling noise came from my bedroom, and I froze.

Oh my gosh! Had we been robbed? Was the robber—or robbers—still in the house? What if somehow, someone knew about my dinosaur egg? What if someone had stolen it?!?!?

I didn't know what to do. Call the police? Run

for help?

Suddenly, a strange screech came from my bedroom, followed by a ferocious chewing sound.

Oh no!

It couldn't have happened, could it? Had the dinosaur egg hatched? It seemed impossible!

Another screech came from my bedroom, then it stopped. No other sounds were heard.

Quietly, cautiously, I crept down the hall. The entire house was a mess. There was junk littered all over the place . . . and my bedroom was the worst.

I leaned forward and peered into my room. A bookshelf had been knocked over, and there were books piled up all over the floor! My boom-box had fallen from my dresser, and it had smashed down onto my CD rack. My CD rack had broken, scattering CD's and CD cases all over the rug.

I flopped on my stomach and peered under my bed, and a surge of terror hit me like a tidal wave.

Beneath my bed, the cardboard box lay in shreds. It had bite marks all over it! Pieces of the egg lay cracked and broken all over the floor!

The dinosaur had hatched!

I stood up, looked down, and gasped, my heart hammering in my chest.

At the floor beneath my window, just to the right of my dresser, was a *hole!* There were bite marks all over the wall around the hole, and pieces of the wall had tumbled to the floor.

The dinosaur had chewed through my bedroom wall, all the way outside!

I dropped to my knees and looked out the gaping hole, searching for the dinosaur. My eyes darted back and forth, across the yard, behind trees and shrubs, across the street.

Nothing. All I could see was green grass, trees, and my neighbor's houses.

And for the first time, the realization of what I had done began to creep through me. The horror spread slowly at first, then built up speed like a charging rhino.

I had brought a dinosaur egg back through time, and the creature had hatched. It actually hatched in a cardboard box in my bedroom!

Worst of all, the dinosaur was loose. He was loose, and he had ripped apart my bedroom and half the house.

The real trouble was about to begin.

I sprang from my house and ran out into the yard, searching for —

For what? I thought. *Just what am I looking for?*

A dinosaur, I supposed. But what kind of dinosaur? A Triceratops? A Stegosaurus?

Nope. It couldn't be a Stegosaurus. They weren't around during the Cretaceous period. Stegosaurus lived during the end of the Jurassic era, about 150 million years ago.

But maybe it wasn't a 'dinosaur' egg, after all. What if it was a Quetzalcoatlus egg?

I looked up, my eyes frantically scanning the sky.

No Quetzalcoatlus.

But then again, if it was a young one, then maybe it couldn't fly yet.

Thoughts were buzzing through my head. Just what, exactly, was I looking for?

I ran across the grass to my bedroom window. A large, green bush below camouflaged the hole. I fell to my knees and searched the ground. The area around the bush consisted of soft dirt, so I thought that maybe I might find—

Footprints.

They weren't very big, and there were only a few, but they were definitely footprints.

Dinosaur footprints.

They were about the size of my feet, with curious claws. A squiggly line seemed to follow the prints in the dirt. Whatever kind of dinosaur it was, it had a tail.

Okay, I thought. *Now we're finally getting somewhere. It's a dinosaur with a tail.*

I leapt to my feet, turned, and scanned the yard, hoping to catch a glimpse of the creature.

Nothing.

I ran around the house to the back yard, but found no trace of the baby dinosaur.

But when I glanced at my watch, I realized I had another problem.

Today was Tuesday. Kristen, my older sister, was spending the next week at her friends' house, so she wouldn't be home. But Mom and Dad bowl on a league every Tuesday evening, and they'd be home any minute—and the house was a disaster!

I ran back inside and got to work. Thankfully, there wasn't anything broken in the house besides some things in my bedroom. A few kitchen chairs had been knocked over, and I stood them up and returned them to their proper places.

The living room was a bit worse, but I managed to straighten it up enough to look okay. A lamp had been overturned and the bulb had blown, so I hastily replaced it and clicked it on and off, making sure that it worked.

So far, so good. Every few seconds I glanced out the window to make sure Mom and Dad weren't pulling in the driveway.

After I straightened up the house, I tackled my bedroom. It was worse than I thought. Not only had the baby dinosaur broken my CD rack and boom-box, but just about everything in the room had bite marks on it! My bedposts had been chewed, and there were claw marks on my dresser!

And, of course, there was the hole in the wall. What was I going to do about that?

I had an idea. I scrambled beneath my bed and pulled out my checker game. I unfolded the checkerboard and placed it over the hole. It covered up the opening, but sooner or later Mom and Dad would find out. How would I explain that?

I'd have to figure that out later—because when I looked outside, I saw Mom and Dad's car in the driveway!

I sprang from my bedroom, closing the door behind me. Dashing from room to room in the house, I double-checked to make sure that I'd picked everything up. Then I sat down on the couch in the living room, picked up the TV remote, and turned the television on—just as Mom was coming in through the front door.

Whew. That had been a close one.

"Hi, Nicky," she said, stepping into the room.

"Mom," I pleaded. "It's 'Nick', not 'Nicky'. Please?" Just recently, Mom had started calling me 'Nicky', and I didn't like it.

"Okay . . . *Nick,*" she laughed, tousling my hair with her hand as she walked past me. "I'll get dinner started. You're probably starving."

◆◆◆

I didn't say much at the dinner table, and I spent the rest of the evening searching the neighborhood for signs of the dinosaur. Summer was at soccer practice, so I was on my own. I suppose I could have asked some of my other friends to help me look, but who would believe me? After all, Mike Parker had laughed when I told him.

No, I would have to search for the baby dinosaur myself.

At eleven o'clock, I gave up. It was dark, and I hadn't seen any sign of the creature. I went back home and said good-bye to Dad, who was getting ready to go to work. Then , I said good-night to Mom, and went to bed. I was tired, and I fell asleep as soon as my head hit the pillow.

But I didn't sleep for long. Sometime, shortly after midnight, I was awakened by a shrill, unearthly shriek in the night!

7

The terrible screeching made me rocket out of a deep sleep. I sat up in the darkness, my heart pounding. My eyes darted about the dark, gloomy room.

Where had the screech come from?

Outside? Yes, that was it. It must have been from outside.

I sat in silence for a moment, listening for the strange noise again. Had Mom heard it? If she did, I'm sure she'd be awake by now.

After about a minute, I got up and tip-toed over to the window. I pulled the drape back.

Our yard was lit up by a single, glowing streetlight. A car was parked near the curb. There was no movement.

But I was certain that I'd heard a screech. Just what it was, I wasn't sure . . . but I had my suspicions.

I suspected it was from the baby dinosaur.

I slipped into my jeans and put on my red and white *Detroit Red Wings* sweatshirt—the one I bought when I went to see a game at Joe Louis Arena. My bedroom door was open just a crack, and I quietly crept into the dark hallway. Mom was still sleeping, I was sure of it. She hadn't heard the screech, after all.

I inched down the hall and through the living room, slowly opening the front door and stepping outside. Our front door makes a loud *thunk!* when it's closed, so I left it open a tiny bit.

Standing on the porch, I froze, listening intently. All I could hear were the usual sounds of the night . . . cars on the distant freeway, horns honking occasionally, and a dog barking here and there.

Suddenly, a crashing sound caught my attention. I turned my head . . . just in time to see a dark shadow darting across the street! It was moving fast, and I couldn't tell what it was. I leapt off the porch and ran across the yard.

At the end of our driveway, two garbage cans had been tipped over. There was garbage strewn everywhere! Torn shreds of paper and food scraps lay tossed about all over the street. Something had ripped into the garbage and really made a mess.

I looked in the direction that I'd spotted the shadow running off.

It could just be a dog, I thought. *Dogs get into our garbage now and then.*

But then again, I didn't really think it was a dog.

I knelt down to inspect the garbage. Most of it had been chewed, and there were visible teeth marks everywhere . . . even on the metal garbage cans! The creature must be hungry!

Well, that would make sense, I thought. *Dinosaurs probably have to eat a lot.*

I rummaged through what was left in the garbage can, and found a steak bone with a little bit of meat on it. I wasn't sure what I was going to do with it, but I figured that if I came across the dinosaur, I could maybe throw it to him.

Which led me to another conclusion. The

dinosaur had gotten into our garbage and was searching for scraps of food—meat! It was a meat eater!

I'm not sure if I liked that idea or not.

Walking slowly in the direction I had seen the shadow, I held out the bone in front of me. I felt a little silly, I guess, walking across the street beneath the light, dangling a small piece of meat in front of me, in hopes of enticing the baby dinosaur—wherever he might be.

In the yard across the street, I stopped and looked around. At night, there sure were a lot of places that a baby dinosaur could hide. Dark shadows provided plenty of areas to remain hidden and unseen.

A sudden noise near a row of shrubs caught my attention and I jumped, surprised by the light shuffling. I froze.

Deep in the shadows, not ten feet from where I stood, a pair of angry, wicked eyes glistened back at me.

I knew right away that the eyes didn't belong to a dog. They were too big, too mean looking. They scowled back at me from the shadows, reflecting the lone streetlight above. The eyes were only a couple feet off the ground, so I imagined the baby dinosaur probably came up to my waist. The creature was too well-hidden in the shadows for me to see his body.

I reached forward and dangled the bone in front of me, contemplating what I would do if the dinosaur actually came out for the bait.

Should I run? Should I drop the bone and back away?

Yes, that's it, I thought. *I'll drop the bone and back up. Slowly. Maybe he'll come out of his hiding place and I'll be able to get a look at him.*

Keeping my eyes on the dinosaur's dark silhouette, I let go of the bone, and it fell to the grass. I took a cautious step back, then another, then another.

Without warning, the dinosaur bolted from the shadows! In a flash, it was upon the piece of meat. It took the bone in its jaws and shook it ferociously, then sprang back to its hiding place.

A stunning realization hit me like a ton of bricks. I stood near the street, my mouth open, my eyes wide. My heart pounded, and I felt dizzy.

I recognized the dinosaur! I would recognize that particular dinosaur *anywhere!* The beady, glaring eyes. The long, vicious teeth. There was no mistake.

It was a Tyrannosaurus Rex. The most barbaric, brutal dinosaur that ever roamed the face of the earth.

But while one part of me was really, really

scared, another part of me was excited! A dinosaur! How cool! Now I could find out all about them . . . *from actual experience!*

I turned and ran across the street and slipped quietly back into my house. In the refrigerator, I found some leftover chicken, some bologna, and some ham. I stuffed the food into a paper bag and went quietly sneaked outside.

I hope you're still there, I thought. *Please be there. Please be in the shadows near the bushes . . . .*

As I approached the place where I'd spotted the T-Rex, a low growl caused me to stop.

Good. Still here. He hadn't run off yet.

I pulled out a chicken leg and waved it in the air.

"Here dinosaur," I whispered quietly. *"Nice dinosaur. Got some chicken for ya. Come on . . . ."*

The baby T-Rex moved. I could hear him shuffling about in the shadows.

Then I could hear sniffing. It sounded like a dog sniffing the air, picking up the scent of food.

Slowly, cautiously, the dinosaur stepped out of the shadows.

It was incredible! The creature looked exactly like what I'd seen in books! It had a thick tail that was about as long as its body. The dinosaur walked upright on his two hind legs. Two smaller, shorter legs were perched up near his chest. His head was big and his mouth was open, showing rows of razor-sharp teeth. Its nostrils flared, and the beast glared at me with shiny, black eyes.

And although I was a little bigger than the dinosaur, I was a bit worried. I would be no match for the creature, should he decide that I would make a nice lunch for him.

I dropped the chicken leg into the grass and took a step back, watching.

The dinosaur swung his head from side to side, sniffing the air. Then he lunged forward with incredible speed, taking the whole chicken bone in his mouth! With a simple crunch and a quick swallow, the chicken leg was gone—bone and all!

The creature turned his attention to me once again, and I reached into the bag, pulling out another piece of chicken. I took another few steps back and dropped the drumstick in the street. My idea was to get the T-Rex to come out beneath the streetlight so I could get a better look at him.

The T-Rex charged for the meat, even before it hit the ground.

"Whoah, dude," I marveled. "You gotta take it easy on the food. I don't have much left."

In the next second, the baby dinosaur had devoured the piece of chicken, and seemed to be waiting for more. I stared at the creature.

He was awesome! In the streetlight, I could see his leather-like skin. It was thick and wrinkled, like an elephant's. I couldn't tell what color he was, but he appeared to be kind of a greenish-gray.

And I knew that the small bit of food that I had brought him wasn't going to be enough. If only . . . .

That's it! I thought. *Mom's got a ton of frozen hamburger in the freezer! The meat is frozen, but maybe the T-Rex would eat it anyway!*

I turned the paper bag upside down, emptying the contents onto the street. The ham and bologna tumbled onto the concrete, and I didn't wait to see if the T-Rex would eat. I wanted to make it to the freezer in the garage and come back, before the dinosaur had slipped away.

I went through the front door and into the kitchen, tip-toeing across the floor to the entry that led out into the garage. I opened the door quietly, strode inside, and turned on the light.

Getting the hamburger to the dinosaur wasn't

very hard. Feeding the dinosaur was the difficult part!

The creature had picked up the scent of the hamburger even before I made it to the street. It was coming toward me! The T-Rex came right into our yard, head held high, nose in the air, sniffing.

I decided that I wasn't going to waste any time. I had a hunk of frozen hamburger in my arms that was the size of a bowling ball. There was more in the freezer, but this might be a good start. I set the piece of meat on the grass and stepped back.

The dinosaur did a curious thing. Instead of viciously attacking the food, he approached warily, slowly, as if he were stalking his prey. He leaned down, sniffed the meat, and licked it. Then, in one single, sudden move, he began chewing at the ball of frozen burger. Small chunks broke off, and the dinosaur ravenously gulped them down.

While the T-Rex ate, I ran back into the garage and grabbed two more hunks of meat. How I was going to explain the missing meat to my mom would be anybody's guess, but I wasn't going to worry about that now. Right now I just wanted to make sure that the baby dinosaur had enough to eat.

I must've fed him ten pounds of hamburger

before he looked like he was full. There was still a small hunk of meat in the grass, but he was eating slower now, making low grunting noises as he chewed. I hate to say it, but he was kind of a pig about the whole thing. Dinosaurs sure don't have good table manners.

Then, without warning, the baby T-Rex leaned back, yawned, leaned forward, and curled up in the grass! He rolled up into a ball, shifted a little bit . . . *and went to sleep!* It didn't take him any time at all. One minute he was on his feet, the next, he was nestled in the grass, sleeping.

I approached guardedly, creeping toward the motionless dinosaur. He looked like a big cat without hair, all cuddled up and asleep. I could see the raising and lowering of his chest as he breathed.

This was awesome! I still couldn't believe I was seeing a real, live dinosaur! No one else in history had ever seen a living dinosaur . . . especially a live T-Rex!

My excitement was short lived . . . because all of a sudden, two bright headlights came out of nowhere. I turned and looked down the street.

Someone was coming! Oh no! They'd spot me — *and the dinosaur* — for sure!

It was a pickup truck. It was moving slowly, and the shadows shortened as it came closer.

What now? I thought. My mind was racing. The baby dinosaur was only a few feet from the curb, and I was standing right next to him.

What if the truck scares the dinosaur and he goes nuts? I wondered. *What if someone in the truck tries to take the dinosaur?*

I turned and looked at the headlights slowly

drawing near. The truck was still a block away, but as it passed beneath a streetlight, I could see a big star-shaped emblem on the side of the door.

Oh no! It was Mr. Mulroony, the dog catcher! He patrols the neighborhood, looking for stray dogs.

And he's not very nice to anyone. He's always scowling, and he looks mad all the time. He wears thick, black-rimmed glasses that are held together on the bridge of his nose with masking tape. Without his glasses, he insists, he's as blind as a bat.

Worst of all, he *hates* dogs. Once, he took Summer's dog, Buster, right out of her front yard! He said it was the law—all dogs outside have to be on leashes. That's crazy! I mean . . . Buster never, ever leaves the yard! Summer had to pay a fine to get him back from the dog pound.

I had to think quick. The truck was getting closer and closer by the second.

The baby T-Rex was still curled up, fast asleep.

Suddenly, I had an idea. I turned and sprang back to our garage. We have a big canvas bag that we use to haul dead leaves in the fall. It's folded up on a shelf in the back of the garage.

I fumbled through the darkness and found it, and took the heavy canvas into my arms. I turned and walked as quickly as I could across the yard.

The truck was still traveling slowly, but it was now only about three houses away. In the next minute, Mr. Mulroony would be right in front of our house.

I quickly unfolded the bag, and placed it right on top of the sleeping dinosaur. I hesitated for a moment when the T-Rex moved a bit, and I thought I had woke him up. He shifted a little, but remained asleep.

I tucked the bag around him so no part of his body was showing, then stepped back. I glanced up at the approaching headlights. If I hurried, I could make it back to the garage without being spotted.

I turned and started to walk, but it was too late. A bright light lit up the yard!

Caught!

I turned back around to see Mr. Mulroony sitting in the truck, pointing a flashlight at me.

"Hey kid," he huffed. "What are you doing out here at this hour?"

Mr. Mulroony knows my name, but he just calls me and all my friends on the block, 'kid'. He's kind of rude.

"Oh, nothing," I replied casually, raising my

arm to shield my eyes from the bright light.

"Someone called to complain about a dog in this area. Making funny noises. You wouldn't know anything about that, would you?"

The dinosaur! I thought. *I'll bet that someone heard the dinosaur screeching and thought it was a dog!*

"Yes," I answered, thinking quickly. "I heard it, too. That's why I got up to come out here. I think—" As I spoke, I swung my arm and pointed with my finger. "—I think it came from the next block over. Division Street, maybe."

Mr. Mulroony turned his head, looking in the direction that I was pointing.

"You sure?" he asked, reaching up with his hand and adjusting his glasses on his nose.

I nodded my head, matter-of-factly. "Pretty sure," I confirmed.

"All right," he replied. "But you go back inside. The person who called said that the dog sounded vicious. It might be dangerous to be out here if there's a wild dog running around."

"Yes, sir," I answered politely.

Mr. Mulroony clicked off the flashlight. The truck began to roll, and I was about to turn and walk back to the house . . . when the truck suddenly stopped again. The flashlight clicked on, illuminating the dark bag in the grass.

"What's that?" Mr. Mulroony asked gruffly.

Gulp!

"Uh, um, uh . . . . " I stammered. I didn't know what to say.

And I certainly couldn't tell him that there was a baby dinosaur beneath the bag!

Just then, I heard the truck door open. Mr. Mulroony got out! He got out of the truck . . . and began walking toward the sleeping dinosaur!

10

There was nothing I could do. In just a few more short steps, Mr. Mulroony would reach the bag. It would take him only two seconds to discover the baby dinosaur hiding beneath the tarp.

Then what would he do? He would capture the T-Rex, I was sure. He would capture it and take it away, and I'd never see it again.

I couldn't let him. I couldn't let him find the dinosaur, and I couldn't let him take the creature away.

Thoughts whirled in my mind. What could I do? How could I stop him?

All of a sudden, I raised my arm and pointed down the block. "There he goes!" I blurted out. "Right there! Over by the Canfield's house!"

Mr. Mulroony stopped in his tracks, and turned to look where I was pointing.

For a moment, we both just stood there, staring off into the distance. Would it work? Would he fall for the oldest trick in the book?

"I don't see anything," he said, adjusting his glasses and cocking his head to one side as he surveyed the area.

"I'm telling you, I saw him!" I insisted. "A big dog! He ran between those two houses over there!"

And right then—a miracle. Because at that exact moment, out of nowhere—a dog barked! It growled and barked from somewhere in the darkness, in the direction that I was pointing! What luck!

Mr. Mulroony forgot all about the bag in the yard, and sprang for his truck. The door slammed closed, and the vehicle sped away. In seconds, I saw the red tail lights of his truck turn a corner and go out of sight.

Wow! That had been a close call.

"You are going to get me into trouble yet," I whispered to the sleeping dinosaur beneath the bag.

But now what would I do? Now that the baby dinosaur was sleeping in the yard, I couldn't just leave him there. Someone would find him in the morning.

And I didn't dare wake him up, either. He might get angry. When I wake my older sister up in the morning, she's like a monster. Teeth and everything.

I decided that I would sit on the porch until the dinosaur woke up. I wasn't sure what I would do then, but maybe I could follow him. Or maybe I could try to catch him. Ideas zipped through my head like race cars.

I walked over to the porch, sat down, and waited.

And waited . . . and waited, and waited.

It wasn't long before I fell asleep, and when I woke up, the baby dinosaur was gone. The baby dinosaur was gone—and a woman across the street was screaming!

11

The sun was just beginning to peek through the trees, and I was groggy from sleep. I'd slept on the porch all night!

The woman's shrill scream stirred me from my deep slumber, and I leapt to the ground and bounded across the grass. I passed the bag that I'd used to hide the dinosaur. The beast was gone, and the canvas was chewed and torn, ripped to shreds!

And now I had another problem. The woman

across the street was still screaming her head off.

I ran across the road and between two houses. The screaming was coming from behind one of the homes, and the woman was really pitching a fit. I turned behind yet another house, and stopped.

A woman wearing a large pink bathrobe stood outside, her gray hair set in curlers. Next to her stood her husband, an equally large man wearing blue sweat pants and a white tank top. He had a thick, caterpillar-like mustache, and his charcoal hair was messy. His hands were on his waist, and he had a tired look of impatience on his face.

"I tell you Harold . . . I saw something! It was a huge lizard, that's what it was! It was mean and ugly and nasty and oh! It was *terrible!*"

I walked toward them, and they turned to look at me.

"Excuse me," I began, "but has anyone seen a big dog this morning?"

The man suddenly threw up his arms. "See, Blanche?!?!" he exclaimed. "Just what I thought. A dog!" Disgusted, the man turned to walk back in his home.

"Well, it sure didn't look like a dog," the woman replied suspiciously. "It didn't look like a dog at all."

Neither person spoke a single word to me, and I laughed under my breath as I walked away.

Smokes! That had been another close one! But I knew it wasn't going to be long before more problems erupted. The baby T-Rex would be constantly searching for food, which meant that he'd be wandering the neighborhood. It was only a matter of time before someone would spot him.

But not if I could help it.

I would need help, and since Summer was with me when I brought the dinosaur egg back through time, she would understand just what had happened.

I sprinted home, took a shower, and changed my clothes. I grabbed a banana, quickly downed a glass of orange juice, and ran out the door.

It only took me a few minutes to bike to Summer's house. She lives on Locust Street, which is several blocks away.

I pounded on the front door of her house, and her little brother came to the door, still wearing his powder blue pajamas. He was holding a *G.I. Joe* doll in one hand, and a small, green, plastic helicopter in the other.

"Travis," I began. "Is your sister home?"

Just then, Summer came out of the hall and into the living room. Travis made a sweeping motion with his toy helicopter and bolted across the room. He sat down on a rug in the middle of the floor, playing with his toys. Summer came to the door and motioned me inside.

"You're here early," she said. "What's up?"

I shook my head. "You're not going to believe me when I tell you," I warned. I nodded to Travis, silently indicating that he probably shouldn't hear what I was going to say.

"Travis, go back to your room and play," she ordered. Without a single word, little Travis got up, plodded across the living room and down the hall. I wished my older sister would listen to me like that.

Summer's eyes lit up. "What is it?" she asked excitedly.

"You know the egg we brought back through time yesterday? It *hatched!* It really hatched!"

I thought Summer was going to fall over.

"You . . . you mean—"

"Yes!" I said. "I got home yesterday, and the whole house was trashed! The dinosaur chewed a hole through my bedroom wall!"

Summer's face turned as white as a sheet.

"What kind is it?" she asked, her voice just above a whisper.

"I'm not absolutely certain," I replied. Although I was pretty sure it was a T-Rex, I wasn't going to tell Summer until I was absolutely positive. "Whatever it is," I continued, "it eats meat."

Her face turned even whiter.

"Are you okay?" I asked. I really thought she was going to faint.

Summer took a deep breath, and the color returned to her face. "Yeah, I'm fine," she replied. "I just can't believe it. I can't believe it really happened. Where is the dinosaur now?"

I shook my head and shrugged my shoulders. "I don't know," I answered. "It's been running around all over my block. The last time I saw him was this morning. That's why I'm here. Can you help me look for him?"

Disappointed, Summer shook her head. "I've got to watch Travis till Mom comes home at noon. I'm stuck."

Rats.

"How about later?" I pleaded.

"Sure," she promised, bobbing her head.

"Cool," I said. "But I need a favor right now.

Do you have any food?"

"Food?" she replied. "Like . . . for what? For the baby dinosaur?"

"You got it," I said. "That little bugger eats anything. Mostly meat. Have you got any meat?"

"Mom's got some steak in the freezer," she replied, nodding toward the kitchen. "But if Dad finds out it's gone, he'll go bonkers. He loves steak."

"I'll replace it before he knows it's gone," I assured her. And I meant it.

Summer hurried to the kitchen and opened the freezer door. She pulled out a big chunk of steak wrapped in white paper, and brought it to me.

"If my dad finds out about this," she warned, handing the meat to me, "he'll flip his lid."

"Don't worry," I pledged, slipping the meat under my arm. "I'll have it replaced in no time."

"What are you going to do?" Summer asked, as I turned to walk out the door.

"I've got to go find that dinosaur before he causes any trouble," I said. "Can you meet me at the pump house after your mom comes home?" The pump house is a building at the end of our block. It's surrounded by a lot of trees and a marsh, and the forest around it is pretty thick. I figured if I was a dinosaur, that would be the place I'd hide.

"Sure," Summer answered, her hand on the door. "It'll be after lunch sometime."

"Good enough," I replied. I hopped off of the porch, leapt onto my bike, and sped home.

I was off to hunt for the baby Tyrannosaurus Rex.

Of course, I didn't know it at the time, but I had more than just *one* dinosaur to worry about.

Soon, I would have *three* to worry about.

12

I scoured the area around the pump house for hours, but I had no luck finding the beast. I found a few of his tracks, but so far, no sign of the creature. I'd even left the slab of steak on a stump, hoping to draw him in.

I waited for what seemed like hours. Every time a branch cracked or a bird chirped, I jumped.

I was sitting on a log, wondering what to do next, when I heard a loud noise in the bushes. My hair stood up on end, and I froze.

He's coming, I thought. *He's here. He's smelled the steak.*

My heart thundered in my chest, and blood rocketed through my veins. But I didn't move a muscle. I didn't dare!

The noise in the bushes grew louder, closer, nearer. I remained motionless, peering into the brush, trying to get a glimpse of the dinosaur.

Suddenly, I saw him! He had stopped in a thick clump of alders, and I could make out his blue skin and his . . . .

Wait a second, I thought. *Blue skin?!?!?* Dinosaurs don't have blue skin!

The bushes parted, and I relaxed.

That's no dinosaur! That's *Summer!*

"Man, you really surprised me!" I exclaimed. "I thought you were the dinosaur."

She was carrying a small grocery bag in her arms, and she looked down at herself. "Yeah, I can see how I might easily be mistaken for one," she replied sharply.

"No, I didn't mean it like . . . I mean . . . oh, forget it. You don't look like a dinosaur."

"Have you seen any sign of him?" she quizzed.

"No," I answered, shaking my head. "But come look at this."

I led her to a place near the marsh where the ground was muddy and soft. "Look," I said, pointing to the ground.

"Wow," she whispered, kneeling down. The dinosaur tracks were clearly visible in the black goo.

"That *has* to be a dinosaur," she speculated. "I've never seen tracks like these before. Ever."

"I wasn't kidding," I said, matter-of-factly. "That dinosaur really hatched. He really hatched — and he's out here somewhere."

Summer stood up, still holding the grocery bag in her arms.

"What've you got?" I inquired, nodding at the brown bag.

"Oh," Summer replied, lowering the bag. She reached in with one arm and pulled out a white package. "Mom said that these spare ribs have been in the freezer too long. She threw them out."

"And you dug them out of the garbage?!?!" I exclaimed.

"Uh-huh," Summer said, nodding her head. "I don't know if your dinosaur eats spare ribs or not, but I figured it was worth a shot."

"I'll bet *this* dinosaur will," I predicted. "I'll bet this dinosaur will eat *anything.*"

I felt now was the time to tell her. I couldn't keep it a secret any longer. Summer needed to know what we were up against, and she needed to know *now*. My eyes met hers, and I spoke.

"I think he's a Tyrannosaurus," I said.

Summer almost dropped the bag. Her mouth opened to speak, but no sound came out. Fear washed over her face.

"We brought a Tyrannosaurus Rex back through time?" she managed to whisper.

I nodded. "Yeah, I'm pretty sure that's what it is," I confirmed.

"But . . . they're like the most ferocious of the dinosaurs!" she gasped. "They'll eat anything! They'll—"

And it was then that we heard the blood-curdling, beastly screech . . . the same screech that had awakened me from a deep sleep last night. It echoed through the trees, this frightening, horrible snarl. The sound made Summer and I jump out of our skins.

"What in the world?!?!?" she cried.

"Over there!" I pointed. "I'll bet that was the baby dinosaur!! On the other side of those trees!"

Summer gasped. "Oh no!" she cried out in horror. "That's the Lorenzo farm!"

She didn't have to say anything more, for I knew what she meant. The Lorenzo's raise horses. Lots of horses.

And I knew that a Tyrannosaurus Rex, when hungry, would eat anything.

Including horses.

13

Disaster was only footsteps away, and I knew it.

Summer dropped the bag of spare ribs and we both sprang through the marsh. My feet made sucking sounds as we plodded through the soft, gooey mud. My white sneakers were now covered with wet muck, but I didn't care.

The only thing I cared about right now was that there were horses in grave danger. Somehow, we had to stop the baby T-Rex.

In seconds, we emerged from the thick stand of trees. A lush, green meadow opened up before us. The field was surrounded by a barbed-wire fence. Off in the distance were a few small sheds, and a very big barn. There were a dozen horses grazing near the barn, chewing grass without a care in the world.

But in the middle of the field, all by itself, stood a small, young foal. It had its head down, its mouth buried in thick grass, chewing.

Summer and I stopped at the barbed wire fence, our eyes scanning the field.

"Over there!" Summer suddenly exclaimed, and I squinted in the sunlight to see what she was looking at.

"I don't see anything," I said, raising my hand above my eyebrows to shield my eyes from the bright sun.

Summer pointed to a clump of weeds in the field. The weeds were tall, and grew close to a large pond.

And then I saw him.

The baby T-Rex. He was hidden in the tall grass, and all I could make out was his head and his beady eyes.

He was watching the foal! The baby T-Rex was

stalking the foal!

I was about to say something like 'we have to stop him' — but it was already too late. At that very instant, the dinosaur sprang.

Summer's whole body stiffened, and she gasped. Both hands flew up to her face, covering her open mouth.

"Oh no!" she shuddered.

There was nothing we could do. The baby Tyrannosaurs Rex tore across the field like lightning, and it was easy to see why this dinosaur had the reputation it did. Mouth open and teeth exposed, it ran low to the ground, faster than a deer, heading straight for the foal.

The tiny horse wasn't going to have a chance.

14

Summer's hands flew up from her mouth, covering her eyes.

"I can't bear to watch!" she shrieked. "This is horrible!"

I felt awful. It was my fault that the dinosaur was here. It would be my fault that an innocent foal was going to lose its life.

The dinosaur picked up speed. It ran with a feverish intensity, focused on its prey. It would only be a matter of seconds now.

Suddenly, the tiny foal saw the dinosaur bearing down. The horse let out a terrified whinny, jumped, turned, and bolted toward the barn— *but the T-Rex didn't follow!*

The baby dinosaur continued running, passing the place where the foal had been grazing. It didn't pay any attention to the small horse at all!

Summer still had her hands over her eyes. She'd heard the horse whinny in terror, and she shuddered, fearing the worst.

"Did he get him?" she choked, holding back her tears.

"No!" I whispered loudly. "Not at all! He's not after the foal! He's after . . . he's after—"

Summer lowered her hands just as the baby dinosaur made an enormous leap over the barbed wire fence. It hit the ground running, sprang across the highway . . . *and attacked a roadside billboard!!*

"Look at that!!" I said.

On the other side of the highway, a blue and green *Burger World* billboard stood. There was a photo of a woman taking a bite out of a huge cheeseburger.

The baby T-Rex leapt off the ground, and face-

planted the cheeseburger on the billboard!

"What on earth . . . ?" Summer exclaimed.

We watched as the baby dinosaur ripped the 'cheeseburger' to shreds! Chips of wood and pieces of paper fell away as the dinosaur chomped viciously at the giant sign. It was actually pretty funny! The baby dinosaur thought the cheeseburger was *real!*

In less than a minute, it was all over. The huge sign was in shambles, and the baby T-Rex had disappeared.

"That's the craziest thing I've ever seen in my life," Summer said, shaking her head.

"Well, I guess we know what it likes to eat," I said.

Summer let out a sigh of relief. "I'm sure glad he doesn't like horses," she said.

We quickly realized we had a tiger by the tail. Without even thinking twice about the consequences, I had brought a dinosaur egg from the past . . . right into the present day. The egg had hatched, and now the dinosaur was alive and loose.

It wasn't fun anymore. This was serious

business.

We had to devise some sort of plan to get the dinosaur back to the Cretaceous period. The window through time would be open for only a few more days, and if we didn't get the baby T-Rex back by then, it would be stuck. *We* would be stuck. I'd probably go to jail for creating such a mess.

Summer and I had searched the area around the billboard, but we found only chewed wood and a few dinosaur footprints. The baby T-Rex was nowhere to be found. We decided that we'd better calm down for a while and think about our problem. I went back to my house, and Summer went back to hers.

We had a problem, all right. I kept thinking about the baby T-Rex, running across the field toward the foal. Even though the dinosaur hadn't been after the small horse, the thought alone was scary. The Tyrannosaurs Rex was—*is*—a vicious, bloodthirsty dinosaur. I knew it was only a matter of time before tragedy struck.

And it was about to . . . much sooner than I'd expected.

15

That night, I found one of my dinosaur books in my bedroom, and sat down to leaf through it. I needed to know everything I could about T-Rex's. I had to know what they hunted, how they hunted, when they hunted. I needed to know when they slept, where they liked to hide, what they didn't like. I needed to know everything. I knew quite a bit already, since we had studied dinosaurs in science class at school.

But I needed to know *more.* This was serious

stuff, now. We had to somehow figure out a way to capture the baby T-Rex, and take it back to the window through time. The 21st century was no place for a meat-eating dinosaur.

I flopped down on my bed, flipped open the book, and began reading. There was so much I needed to know, so much I needed to learn. I had heard so much about the Tyrannosaurus Rex, and how it had been the most feared dinosaur of its time. The T-Rex would stop at nothing to fill its appetite.

The sharp trill of the telephone disturbed my studying, and then Mom popped her head inside my bedroom.

"Nicky? Summer is on the phone for you."

I rolled my eyes. "It's *Nick*, Mom. Remember? *Nick.*"

"That's right," she apologized. "Nick it is." She disappeared.

I placed my dinosaur book on the bed and went into the living room. The portable phone was on the coffee table, and I quickly snatched it up.

"Hey," I began. "What's up?"

"I have an idea to catch the baby dinosaur!" Summer said anxiously. "And it just might work!"

"You do?!?! Cool! Can you come over?" I

asked.

"Give me ten minutes," Summer replied, and she hung up the phone.

◆◆◆

I went outside and sat on the porch to wait. It had grown dark, and lights glowed in houses across the street and down the block. Several crickets chirped from nearby, and, a few houses over, a group of unseen adults were laughing and talking. A siren wailed in the distance.

Ten minutes later, right on the button, I saw the Summer dark silhouette as she walked quickly toward my house. She was carrying a bag, just like earlier today.

I got up from the porch, and dashed to the curb to meet her. We met beneath a glowing street light.

"What were you saying about an idea to catch the baby T-Rex?" I asked.

"Well, we can use these cheeseburgers," she began, glancing at the bag under her arm. "I bought twelve of them at *Burger World*. Here's what I'm thinking:

"My dad bought a snowmobile last winter. It

came in a big crate made out of wood. He's always meant to throw out the box, but never has. It's still sitting behind our garage.

"We could make a trap for the dinosaur by propping the crate up with a stick. We'll tie a string around a couple cheeseburgers, and attach the other end of the string to the stick."

A light bulb clicked on in my head. I'd seen that kind of trap before. "And when the baby T-Rex picks up the cheeseburger," I said excitedly, "he'll pull the string!"

Summer nodded. "Right! The string will pull the stick, and the box will fall—capturing the dinosaur inside!"

"That might work!" I said. "But where are we going to set the trap?"

"In our back yard behind our steel shed. It's dark there, and I don't think anyone will see. Besides . . . the wood box is heavy. I don't think we'd be able to carry it too far."

"Let's go set it up right now," I said anxiously. "We can't wait a minute more. The sooner we have the baby T-Rex captured, the better."

"Have you seen it since earlier today?" Summer asked, as we walked down the sidewalk beneath the street lights.

"Nope," I replied, shaking my head. "But I haven't been looking for him, either."

We continued walking, both of us wondering where the baby T-Rex might be.

Of course, what we didn't know was that the baby T-Rex knew where *we* were. He'd already caught wind of the tantalizing, delicious aroma of cheeseburgers in Summer's arms — and the beast was stalking us at that very moment.

16

It was Summer who noticed it first.

We were almost to her house when she slowed, turning her head from left to right. She stopped walking, and I did, too.

"What?" I asked.

"Don't you feel it?" she asked curiously, her eyes scanning the dark shadows around trees and houses.

"Feel what?" I replied, looking around.

"I don't know," she said quietly. Her voice was tense and tight. "It's like . . . like we're being watched."

I continued to scan the yard and the houses. It was getting late, and there were no other cars on the street. Most of the homes on the block had lights on, but there were a few that buildings that were completely dark.

But I didn't see anything. And I didn't feel anything, either. At least, I didn't feel like we were being watched.

"Come on," I urged confidently, and I began walking again. "It's getting late. We've got to get that trap set. Tonight."

Summer was a bit apprehensive. She stood motionless, her head darting nervously from side to side, searching.

"You're right," she finally agreed. "It's probably nothing. Let's go get that trap set."

We hadn't gone twenty feet when a low, deep snarl stopped both of us dead in our tracks.

"D . . . did . . . did you h . . . hear . . . hear that?" I stammered.

"Yes," Summer whispered. "It's him, isn't it?"

I was about to speak when Summer received

her answer. There was a slow movement between two houses, and we peered into the shadows to get a look.

But I was already sure what it was. No dog could growl like that. That sound could only come from the most vicious, barbaric of the dinosaurs — a Tyrannosaurus Rex.

Suddenly, two glassy eyes appeared. The baby dinosaur had taken a few steps toward us, and we could see the outline of his head silhouetted in the darkness.

"Looks like he found us before we found him," I whispered.

"It's the cheeseburgers!" Summer said. "He smells the cheeseburgers!"

Summer held the bag of burgers tightly beneath her arm. She held them close to her, as if she was protecting them. I wasn't sure if that was such a good idea.

I mean, if the baby T-Rex decided that he wanted the burgers, he wasn't going to let Summer get in the way. The thought scared me. Summer was my friend. I didn't want to see anything happen to her.

"Summer," I instructed quietly, "hand me the

bag. Real slow and gentle. Hand the cheeseburgers to me."

"What are you going to do?" she asked.

"Never mind. Just give me the bag."

Both of our eyes remained fixed on the shadow of the dinosaur between the houses. I took a slow step toward Summer, and she handed me the bag. I reached out and took it, then pulled it close.

Got it! Now, if the dinosaur attacked, at least Summer would be safe. Sure, I might get ripped to shreds, but Summer would be okay.

"Nick, What are you going to do?" Summer asked again.

Truthfully, I didn't know. I just wanted the bag of cheeseburgers away from Summer so it would get her out of danger. What I was going to do now, I hadn't a clue.

But whatever I was going to do, I'd better do it quick . . . because suddenly, without warning, the dinosaur sprang from the shadows—and he was headed straight for me!

17

The baby T-Rex sprang so quickly, I hardly had time to react. And I did the only thing I could think of.

In one quick movement my hand shot into the bag of cheeseburgers. I grabbed one and yanked it out, wound my arm up like a major-league baseball pitcher, and threw it at the charging dinosaur with all of my might. I didn't know if I was trying to hit the dinosaur of simply distract him . . . but at the moment, I didn't care. I just wanted to buy us some time so we might be able to get away.

The cheeseburger flew through the air, and my aim wasn't very good. As soon as I let it fly, I could tell that I would miss the beast by a mile.

Or so I thought.

The moment the burger left my fingers, the baby dinosaur had it in his sights. He seemed to know where it was going, how fast, and where it would land.

As a result, the T-Rex changed direction, storming after the airborne morsel with lightning speed. He snapped his head up, and, in one quick motion, snared the cheeseburger in its mouth!

But regardless how bad my aim had been, the plan worked . . . because it stopped the dinosaur from charging.

"Summer," I said quietly as the dinosaur chewed. "Go home. Go inside. I'll be there in a minute."

"No way," Summer insisted from behind me. "I'm not leaving here without you."

I didn't have time to argue. The baby T-Rex had gulped down the cheeseburger, wrapper and all, and began lunging toward us once again.

I reached my hand into the bag and let another

cheeseburger fly. My aim was better this time, and the dinosaur stopped, snared the burger from the air, and began chewing. Before he was finished I had grabbed another one, ready to throw it in an instant.

Summer had crept up right behind me, and I could hear her breathing over my shoulder.

"He's . . . he's actually kind of cute," she said.

The dinosaur finished the burger and took another few steps toward us.

I decided to try something.

I held out the cheeseburger so he could see it. When it caught his attention, I began to move my arm, swinging the burger from left to right.

The baby dinosaur stopped, his head following the movement of the cheeseburger.

"Watch this," I whispered, and I gently tossed the cheeseburger, underhand, to the dinosaur. The T-Rex caught it expertly, chomping and chewing, swallowing it in seconds. Only this time, after it finished eating, it didn't come toward us. It stayed right where it was, waiting.

"Now watch," I said. Slowly . . . very, very slowly . . . I took a step — *toward the baby T-Rex!*

"What are you doing?!?!?" Summer cried out in a hoarse whisper. *"You're going to get torn to*

pieces!!!!"

I didn't answer her. I was concentrating too hard on what I was doing.

The dinosaur remained where he was, motionless except for his tail. It swung back and forth like the tail of a cat, waiting, expecting.

Hunting.

I gently tossed another burger to the beast, and again, he snapped it out of mid-air.

I took another step forward. I was only an arm's-length from the dinosaur now. I could probably feed him from my hand if I wanted.

Did I dare? Should I try and get the dinosaur to take a cheeseburger right out of my hand?

Only two things could happen. He could take the cheeseburger and eat it . . . or he could take the cheeseburger, as well as my whole hand.

But I didn't think he would.

Slowly, carefully, I reached into the bag and pulled out another cheeseburger. The bag was getting low, and there were only a couple more cheese-burgers left. I held out the bit of food, urging the dinosaur to come closer.

I've got to say that this was the most incredible experience of my life. Right before me, just a few feet away, was a dinosaur that was from the Cretaceous era . . . 70 million years ago! I took a long, hard look at the incredible creature before me.

His skin was rippled and rough, and his nostrils flared as he sniffed the air. Behind him, his fat tail swished methodically back and forth, waiting, calculating. His deep, black eyes glared back at me as I held out the cheeseburger.

He was waiting.

He was in no hurry.

This was the Tyrannosaurus Rex at the core. The beast knew, even at his young age, that he would snare the cheeseburger. He would have the cheeseburger whether I decided to toss it to him, or if he had to rip it out of my hands.

Yet he chose to wait—for the time being.

Perhaps he was stalking the cheeseburger, waiting for just the right moment.

Or maybe he was stalking me. I couldn't tell.

"Nick . . . ." Summer whispered urgently from behind me. Her voice was filled with terror and worry.

"Sshhhh," I assured her quietly. "I'll be fine."

I sure hoped I was right.

I swished the cheeseburger back and forth in

front of the T-Rex, and his watchful eyes followed the movement.

I moved closer, bringing the cheeseburger closer to his nose.

As the baby T-Rex lurched forward to take the burger, I pulled back slowly. The dinosaur crept forward, cautiously, reaching, stretching . . . .

There! He was so close, I could smell his breath on the skin of my arm.

And boy . . . did he stink!

As he leaned forward, I let him have the cheeseburger, dropping it into long, razor-sharp teeth.

Wow! I thought. *I'm the only person in the world who has ever fed a T-Rex from their hands! A real, live T-Rex! Too cool.*

But there was a problem. I was down to just three cheeseburgers! What would happen when I ran out? I'd worked so hard to get the baby T-Rex to eat out of my hand . . . but what would I do when I had nothing more to feed him? What would *he* do? What if he was still hungry?

Whoops. I guess I hadn't thought of that.

Very slowly, I pulled out one of the remaining cheeseburgers, held it out toward the T-Rex, then tossed it in the grass a few feet away. The dinosaur was upon the morsel in an instant, and I took several steps backward while the T-Rex chewed.

Two cheeseburgers left.

I reached into the bag and pulled one out.

"When I throw this one, get ready to make a break for it," I whispered to Summer.

"Make a break for it?!?! To where?!?!" Summer replied.

"I don't know. Just . . . just get ready to run. Okay?"

"Okay," Summer agreed.

The baby T-Rex had just finished the cheeseburger, and he turned his attention to us.

I raised the burger up so he could see it in my hand, then drew it back and let it fly. It soared high above the T-Rex, and the beast's head tilted back, following the flying yellow wrapper as it careened overhead. The burger arched and began to fall, finally plopping down into a darkened yard. It bounced once and rolled to a stop.

The T-Rex suddenly let out a screech and bolted after the burger, and Summer and I spun and took off running toward her house. We didn't have far to go, but we weren't taking any chances. Both of us ran as fast as our legs would take us.

But alas, it wasn't fast enough, for in the next instant I found myself tumbling to the ground. The cheeseburger bag flew from my hands and I hit the ground with a heavy thud. The single, last burger spilled out, and tumbled away. My face was planted firmly in the grass, and I could hear Summer screaming.

My plan hadn't worked! I had been attacked, knocked to the ground by the charging T-Rex!

18

Strong, vice-like claws dug into my shoulder. The T-Rex was heavy, and I was forcefully pinned to the ground. I tried to scream, but the creature had knocked the wind from me, and I struggled to catch my breath.

And when I heard Summer scream, I knew that it was all over.

I was fighting as hard as I could to get away, but it was no use. I could only wait until the huge, razor-sharp teeth plunged into my neck.

I was a goner.

All of a sudden, the weight was off of me. The dinosaur had jumped off!

I had a chance to get away, and I didn't waste any time. I rolled sideways, leapt to my feet, and bolted.

"Hold it!" a strange voice commanded. The voice was close by. I stopped.

Wait a minute—I hadn't been attacked by the baby T-Rex, after all!

When I turned, I saw a big kid getting to his feet. He looked like he was about seventeen or eighteen years old.

And in the bone-white glow of the street light, I could tell he was *mad.*

"Caught you in the act, you little vandal!" he hissed.

Vandal?!?!?! Who? ME?

"What are you talking about?" I demanded. I had finally caught my breath, but my heart was pounding like a pile driver.

"You're the kid that's been letting the air out of my car tires every night, aren't you?!?!?" He was really angry, and he clenched his fists and took another step toward me.

"No, he's not!" Summer intervened.

"Somebody's been letting the air out of my car tires every night," the guy said. "And I'll bet that it's *you*."

"That's a bet you'd lose," I replied, shaking my head. "Somebody might be letting the air out of your tires, but it isn't *me*."

The guy glared at me. I hoped he believed me. He was big enough to pound me into the ground like a golf tee!

"Well, then, what are you doing out this late?" he demanded.

"We're feeding a dinosaur," Summer said sarcastically. "What does it look like?"

"Yeah, right," the guy said. He looked at Summer, then back at me. "If I catch you letting the air out of my tires, you're in for it." He spun on his heels, and walked across the street.

"Wow," I breathed. "I almost got my face mashed." I watched his shadow as he walked up a nearby driveway and into a darkened garage.

But now we had another problem: the baby dinosaur was nowhere to be found.

The T-Rex was gone.

19

We walked to the yard where the T-Rex had attacked the cheeseburger. There was no sign of the dinosaur, except some tear marks in the grass from his claws, and a few yellow shreds of wax paper.

Summer and I turned our heads, searching dark yards and gloomy shadows. The T-Rex couldn't be far. We canvassed the yards and bushes around nearby houses.

After a few minutes of unsuccessful searching,

we gave up.

"Come on," Summer said. "He's can't be too far. This will give us time to set up our trap."

We jogged the rest of the way to Summer's house. There were a few lights on in her home, and Summer ran inside to tell her mom that she had returned. She came back outside a moment later with a flashlight and a nylon rope.

"This will be perfect," she said, holding up the white rope. "We'll tie one end to the stick, and one end to the bait. When the dinosaur eats the food, he'll pull the rope, which will then pull the stick, and the box will fall down on top of him."

"What are we going to use as bait?" I asked. I knew we'd have a hard time trying to tie a cheeseburger to a rope!

Summer thought about it for a moment, then walked over to a big freezer in the garage. She lifted the lid, and the freezer light came on, sending eerie shadows flying in the darkness. Inside the freezer were a lot of white packages with different dates written on them. She picked up one of the packages, inspected it for a moment, then gave it to me. She closed the freezer.

"If my mom finds out that I used that steak, I'm

110

in for it," she whispered.

"Hey," I said. "I've already fed your dad's steak to the T-Rex. I won't tell if you won't tell." I made a zipping motion over my lips, and Summer giggled.

We walked around the house to a shed in Summer's back yard. It sure was dark! Summer clicked on the flashlight, and waved the beam on the grass before us.

Behind the shed was a huge crate made of wood. The slats were spaced apart, so we could see through the box. That would help. If our plan worked, we'd be able to see the baby dinosaur through the crate without having to lift it up.

Holding the flashlight to her body with her arm, Summer unwrapped the piece of meat with both hands. It was pink and slimy.

"Tie the rope around the entire piece," she ordered, holding the meat up to the light. "Tight. Make sure that the dinosaur has to tug at it to eat it."

I wrapped the nylon rope around the hunk of meat twice, then tied it tight. I pulled on the rope to make sure that the meat wouldn't slip off easily.

Summer took the rope from my hand and lowered the meat to the ground. She swung the flashlight beam ahead of her, illuminating the wood crate.

"Come on," she said. "Let's see if we can lift it."

I was surprised at how heavy the box really was. It took both of us to lift it. When we finally had lifted one end high enough, I propped the stick under it. When the box was braced up, I picked up the meat and tied the other end of the rope to the stick.

"There," I said, standing up. "That should do it."

The trap was set. All we had to do was wait.

But it was getting late, and I had to go home. Man, I wished I could've stayed!

"I've got to head back," I said reluctantly. "But call me first thing in the morning. I've got to know what happens."

Summer promised she would, and said good-bye.

I ran all the way home, took a shower, and went to bed—not knowing that when I woke up, things weren't going to go as planned.

The city of Detroit was about to be turned upside down.

20

That night, before I went to bed, I decided not to wait until Summer called. I set my alarm, and got up at five the next day.

The sky outside was just beginning to lighten in the east, and the early morning air was cool as I rode my bike past rows of houses. I could hear cars stream by on the freeway not far away, and an occasional horn blared once in a while.

After a few minutes, I arrived at Summer's

house. It was still kind of dark, and there were no lights on. I hopped off my bike, pushed it around to the back yard, leaned it up against the garage, and walked toward the shed.

But even before I reached the trap, I could see that it had worked.

The crate had fallen! We'd caught the dinosaur!

I crept forward cautiously, my sneakers sinking into the damp, dew-covered grass. I stopped a few feet away, peering through the wood slats.

There was something there! I could see the dark shape of the caged T-Rex.

We caught him! I thought excitedly. *We really caught him!*

As I approached the trap, the beast stirred. I could see his shadow shifting nervously about within the cage.

Suddenly, the shadow within the cage let out a low growl—and *barked!*

For crying out loud, I thought, my excitement fading. *We didn't catch a dinosaur! We caught a stray dog!*

Great. Some dinosaur catchers we turned out to be.

The dog didn't appear to be mean, so I lifted the corner of the crate. It took everything I had to lift it, but as soon as the huge box was off the ground just a few inches, the dog stuck his head out from beneath, and wriggled free. He took of running and never looked back.

"Sorry about that, bud," I said quietly to the fleeing dog. I wondered how long he'd been cooped up in the box. Probably most of the night.

All day long we searched for the baby T-Rex, but our efforts were fruitless. We came across a few tracks down near the pump house, but nothing more.

Where had the dinosaur gone? We spent the whole day looking for him, without any sign. Finally, right around dinner time, we gave up. Summer went home, and I went to my room.

I had several more books about dinosaurs, and I flipped through them. I needed to know as much as possible about the Tyrannosaurus Rex. What they ate, where they slept, stuff like that. Maybe that would give me some clues as to where we'd find the baby.

I read a lot of interesting things. I read that scientists speculated that the T-Rex couldn't move very fast, compared to other dinosaurs. Which was strange, because the baby T-Rex we'd brought back from the Cretaceous era was like lightning! Maybe they get slower when they get older, like my dad.

I spent the rest of the evening poring through my books. I got on the internet on Mom's computer and looked up every website I could find that had information about dinosaurs. Then I went back into my room to go through my dinosaur books again.

We were really in trouble. The T-Rex is a vicious, terrible beast, and the more I read, the more my heart sank.

What if we didn't find him? I thought. *What if he gets hungry and starts eating other things besides cheeseburgers? Things like—*

I didn't want to think about it. My mind was already whirling and swirling, trying to think of what to do. Every minute that ticked by was another minute that the dinosaur was loose in the streets.

And so, when I heard the noise at my window, I jumped.

And when I saw the baby T-Rex clawing at the screen, I just about fainted.

21

Terror rushed through me, and I was paralyzed by fear. My whole body began to shake.

But what's more: the face of the T-Rex began to change! It began to twist and turn, its features distorting and looking more like . . . .

Like—

Summer!

And the creature began to *talk!* Its mouth was moving as it spoke to me!

"Nick!" it was saying. "Nick! Let me in!"

That's when I woke up—and discovered Summer standing outside my bedroom window.

Whew! It was only a nightmare! I must've fallen asleep while reading my dinosaur books.

I stood up, strode to the window, and opened it up.

"Man," I said, shaking my head. "You sure scared me. I thought you were the dinosaur! I thought you were trying to break in to eat me!"

But Summer wasn't listening. Her eyes were bulging, and she had an expression of fear on her face. She looked like she was about to explode like an over-filled balloon.

"Nick!" she blurted out. *"Dinosaurs! Real dinosaurs! They've attacked Detroit!!"*

Huh? Had Summer flipped or something? What was she saying?

"Relax," I said. "We only brought back the one egg. There aren't any other dinosaurs around."

"Didn't you say that the window through time will be open for exactly seven days?!?!?"

"Yeah, sure," I replied. "That's what my grandpa said, anyway."

"Well, wouldn't that mean that dinosaurs would be able to come *through* the window themselves? I mean ... what if they stumbled upon the window ... and climbed through?"

Impossible, I thought.

But there was something inside of me that began to tremble.

"Come in through the front door," I instructed, "and tell me what you're talking about."

She disappeared and I spun, hurrying out of my bedroom and into the living room. For the first time, I noticed that it was morning. I'd slept all night on my chair in my bedroom!

It was early, and Mom was still sleeping. I let Summer in through the front door, and she immediately ran across the living room to the TV. She picked up the remote, and the television screen blinked to life. The news was on.

And what they were talking about was the most incredible, unbelievable thing I had ever heard in my life.

Dinosaurs ... real, live, dinosaurs ... *HUGE ones* ... were attacking the city of Detroit!

22

It was like watching a horror movie. There was smoke and fire everywhere. Entire *buildings* had been knocked to the ground. I couldn't believe that the images I was seeing on the screen were real!

But by far the most horrifying images were the dinosaurs.

Tyrannosaurs. There were two of them ravaging downtown Detroit, smashing cars and demolishing buildings. Sparks flew when one of the huge beasts smashed a power transformer. It was like I was watching a *Godzilla* movie — only worse!

"*The dinosaurs seemed to come from out of nowhere,*" the TV reporter's voice was saying. "*We have reports that the T-Rex's have smashed dozens of cars and wrecked over thirty buildings in a two block radius. Just where these dinosaurs came from is anybody's guess . . . but one thing is for sure . . . it's total chaos in downtown Detroit today. Total chaos.*"

Gulp.

I continued watching, my fear growing with every passing second. The dinosaurs were truly hideous creatures, and nothing in their path was safe. Cars went tumbling as the enormous beasts stomped and kicked their way down the street . . . two blocks from Joe Louis Arena! It was like watching a bizarre science-fiction movie on television.

"*And what's even stranger,*" the reporter continued, "*is that the dinosaurs appear to be looking for something. We've been watching the T-Rex's as they travel, and they definitely appear to be searching for something.*"

I saw stars. Things got fuzzy, my knees shook, and I almost fell forward. I thought I was going to pass out.

"*The baby,*" I stammered quietly.

Summer turned her head and stared into my eyes. "I knew you were going to say that," she said. Her voice was strained, and filled with terror.

We continued watching TV, both of our eyes glued to the television screen.

How was I supposed to know? I thought. I couldn't have known that I was taking a Tyrannosaurs Rex egg. I just thought it was a plain old, ordinary dinosaur egg from the Cretaceous era. I didn't know it was a T-Rex egg! I didn't know it would hatch! And I sure didn't think that Mom and Dad T-Rex would come looking for their baby!

We were in deep trouble.

Well, I was, anyway. This hadn't been Summer's idea. She had just gone along to see if there really was a 'window through time.' I was the one who insisted on bringing the dinosaur back to the present.

"I've been reading about Tyrannosaurs," Summer said, her eyes still glued to the television screen. "I read that they have a great sense of smell. Better than a dog's, even."

I knew what she was getting at. The dinosaurs had emerged from the window through time . . . which was miles from where we lived.

But with their keen sense of smell, it was only

a matter of time before they picked up the scent of their baby . . . which was somewhere, roaming our neighborhood.

The two Tyrannosaurs would be headed right for our block.

23

I can't describe just how terrified I was at that moment, watching the television. The two beasts were storming down streets while cars quickly shot off in all directions, trying to escape the horrible creatures. One of the beasts stepped on a moving truck, and the driver hopped out and ran, just seconds before the T-Rex came down with all of his weight, squishing the truck like a bug.

"We've got to find the baby T-Rex!" I said to

Summer. "We've got to find him, and somehow take it back to the window through time before it's too late!"

"Nick . . . look at the TV!" Summer cried, pointing. "It's *already* too late! Look at what the dinosaurs are doing to Detroit!"

"But we can't just stand here and do nothing," I said. "If we do, it'll just be a matter of time before the dinosaurs follow the scent of their baby to our neighborhood! All of our homes will be wiped out!"

It was hard to take our eyes off the glowing television screen. The two dinosaurs continued their thundering waltz through the city, smashing buildings and ripping up entire blocks. A helicopter swooped overhead, but it was almost smashed to smithereens when one of the T-Rex's snapped at it with its huge, powerful jaws. The copter spun and swung back and out of reach of the lunging dinosaur, just in time.

I hastily scribbled a note for Mom to let her know I'd be riding my bike.

"Come on!" I ordered. I spun and ran into the garage. Summer followed.

"What?" she asked anxiously. "What are you thinking?"

My bicycle was propped against the wall in the

garage, and I jumped on it.

"I think I know how we can catch the baby T-Rex!" I answered. Summer climbed on her bike, and we rode out the driveway while I explained my idea.

"The baby dinosaur likes cheeseburgers, right?" I reasoned, weaving my bike out of the driveway and onto the sidewalk.

"Yeah," Summer agreed, her blonde hair flying in the wind.

"Well, if we can attract him with a few cheeseburgers, maybe we can lead him back to the window through time," I continued. "Maybe we can lead him back . . . and the other two T-Rex's might follow his scent—"

"—right back through the window through time!" Summer blurted.

"Hopefully," I finished. My breath was heavy from pedaling my bike so hard. "It's a long shot. But we've got to try. How much money do you have?"

"Not a lot," Summer replied. "Maybe five dollars. And a twenty dollar bill that I've been saving since last Christmas."

"We're going to need it," I said, turning down another street. "I've got a few dollars on me now. That'll get us about a half dozen cheeseburgers. I'll go get them at Burger World, and meet you at your house. But you'll need to get your money so we can get more food for the baby T-Rex. Six cheeseburgers aren't going to last very long."

The plan sounded crazy. Last week, if you would have told me that I would be buying cheeseburgers to feed a real, live dinosaur, I would've laughed my head off.

It sure didn't seem funny now.

Summer turned down another side street and headed for her home, while I pumped my bicycle furiously toward the fast-food restaurant.

Thankfully, *Burger World* wasn't very busy. I got some strange looks when I rode up to the drive-thru window on my bicycle, but I didn't care. I had other things to worry about. I had to beg and plead with the server at *Burger World* to make some cheeseburgers for me. He said that all they were making was muffins and other breakfast items, and wouldn't be cooking burgers for several hours.

"Please?" I begged. Behind me, a car honked impatiently. "It's an emergency," I said. And it was. Reluctantly, he agreed to make some cheeseburgers for me.

It took me ten minutes to bike to Summer's house. She was waiting for me in her driveway, her arms resting on the handlebars of her bicycle.

"I've got seven cheeseburgers," I stated. "It's not much, but it's a start. Come on. We've got to find that little bugger."

We rode back to my house, searching behind houses and in bushes—anywhere we thought the baby Tyrannosaurus Rex could hide. We scoured the neighborhood, but again, we found no sign of the young dinosaur.

What had happened? Had the baby picked up the scent of his parents? Maybe the dinosaur was looking for the two other T-Rex's. Was the young T-Rex still in the neighborhood?

We searched all day, trying to find the baby T-Rex, but we didn't have any luck. We skipped lunch, and Mom made lasagna for dinner. Dad, of course, was sleeping, since he works overnight. Mom and I ate and watched TV. On every channel, they were talking about the dinosaurs. Mom couldn't believe it.

After dinner, I rode over to Summer's house, and we began our search again. Finally, after finding no sign of the baby dinosaur, we gave up. It was almost ten o'clock, and we decided to leave the cheeseburgers placed in different areas around the block. Hopefully, if the baby T-Rex was still around, he'd pick up the scent of the cheeseburgers. We'd know in the morning.

But we had one big problem that I didn't want to think about.

Tomorrow was Monday. It would be exactly seven days since the window through time had opened. At exactly 3:05 tomorrow afternoon, the window through time would close. If we didn't find the baby T-Rex and lead him back to the window through time by then, he'd be stuck here.

Along with two fully-grown, man-eating, dinosaurs.

Things weren't looking good—and they got worse at exactly six-thirty the next morning when the doorbell rang.

24

I heard the loud *ding-dong* from my bedroom, and I heard Mom get up to go to the door.

It was Mr. Mulroony, the dog catcher! I could hear his angry voice from my bedroom. I crept out of bed and tip-toed over to my bedroom window. The window was open, and I could hear Mr. Mulroony speaking.

"Did you see anything?" he was asking. "That darn dog sure tore up the neighborhood last night."

Mom answered him, but I couldn't hear what she said.

"Well, if you see him, you give me a call, will ya?"

Mom again said something to him, and Mr. Mulroony stepped off the porch and walked to his idling truck.

It was then that I noticed the yard.

And the street.

And the neighbor's yards.

Garbage had been strewn everywhere! During the night, the baby T-Rex must've ripped into every garbage can on the block! The street looked like a dump. Papers, empty cans, bottles, and other debris littered the road and the yards. There were a few people outside wandering about, just shaking their heads.

I heard a noise behind me, and I turned. Mom was standing in my bedroom doorway.

"You *are* awake," she said, pushing the door all the way open. "Good morning."

"Hi," I said, glancing back outside. I couldn't believe the piles of litter all over the place.

"Some mess out there, huh?" she said. I nodded my head, already knowing what she was going to ask.

◆◆◆

Cleaning up the yard and the driveway took a good half-hour. Mom had said that Mr. Mulroony was madder than a wet hen when he'd received the phone call, complaining about the dog that had ripped through everyone's garbage. Mr. Mulroony told my mom that he was going to get that dog if it was the last thing he was going to do.

And he was right. If he happened to catch this 'dog', it just might be the last thing that he would do!

After I finished picking up the garbage, I went back inside. Mom was watching the news on television. The reporter was saying that the dinosaurs had moved through downtown, and were making they're way farther into the suburbs. Livonia, Westland, and many other surrounding cities were in danger. Thankfully, the huge Tyrannosaurs weren't real close to where we live.

Still, no one had figured out where the beasts had come from — and worse, no one knew how to stop them. A police officer was interviewed, and he was saying that they had shot one of the dinosaurs with over twenty tranquilizers, but they hadn't had any effect on the huge creature!

"Can you believe that?" Mom exclaimed, shaking her head. "It's incredible!"

"Yeah, it's bizarre, all right," I agreed. "I hope they don't come any closer."

Amazingly, no one had been seriously hurt. The authorities had been tracking the dinosaurs, and they'd been able to warn people in time for them to leave their homes and offices.

I called Summer's house. Her mom answered, and said that Summer was still sleeping.

"Mrs. McCready," I pleaded, "this is important. I really need to talk to her."

"Okay," she replied. "Hang on."

I waited for what seemed like hours. Summer was groggy when she came to the phone.

"H . . . hello?" she croaked.

"Summer," I said quietly. I didn't want Mom to hear what I was saying. *"Our yard . . . and the whole neighborhood . . . is a mess. The baby T-Rex was here last night . . . and he ripped up the garbage again."*

There was a pause on the other end of the phone.

"I'll be there in ten minutes," she said finally.

I looked at the clock. It was almost eight, and Dad would be home soon.

But most importantly, we had only seven hours to find the baby T-Rex .... and somehow rescue the city of Detroit from the angry wrath of two prehistoric monsters.

This wasn't a game. It wasn't fun. What began as an exploration of the window through time, had become a chaotic mess.

And if we didn't somehow get the dinosaurs back to the Cretaceous era, things would get worse.

A *lot* worse.

We had a mere seven hours. That was it.

Impossible, I thought. Seven hours to save the entire city of Detroit.

There was no time to lose.

25

Just like she'd promised, Summer arrived at my house ten minutes after I'd hung up the phone. We wasted no time searching the neighborhood.

Evidence of the baby T-Rex was everywhere. In several places, we found the tell-tale track marks in soft dirt. It was the dinosaur that was responsible for tearing into everyone's garbage, all right.

But even more importantly, the cheeseburgers were gone. There was no sign of them at all.

"Do you still have that twenty bucks?" I asked Summer.

She stuffed her hands into her jeans pocket and pulled out a rumpled bill.

"Okay," I began. "We've got to be ready. If we see the baby T-Rex, we'll need to have an arsenal of cheeseburgers. We'll try to lead him back to the field — and back to the window through time."

We rode our bikes to *Burger World*. This time we went inside, and boy . . . did we get some funny looks when we ordered twenty-seven cheeseburgers!

But most people didn't pay attention to us. There were a lot of customers at the restaurant, and they were swarming around the two televisions that hung from the wall. They were watching — you guessed it — *the dinosaurs!* Summer and I waited in line, looking at the crowd of people near the TV screens.

"Uh . . . " the guy behind the counter said as Summer handed him the twenty. "Do you want any fries with your order?"

I shook my head. All we needed were cheeseburgers. He handed me the over-sized bag, and I took it with both hands.

Summer and I were hurrying toward the door when a sudden gasp swept through crowd of people.

We turned.

"*Oh my gosh!*" Summer whispered.

On TV, the two dinosaurs could clearly be seen from an angle high in the sky. The camera person was in a helicopter, filming the bizarre scene below.

The two dinosaurs were attacking the Fisher building! Smoke and fire billowed out from windows, and chunks of metal and glass and mortar were flying everywhere!

The unseen reporter on TV was frantic. "*This is madness, ladies and gentlemen, complete madness!*" He seemed on the verge of crying. "*The two dinosaurs have attacked the Fisher building, and it appears they may succeed in toppling the entire structure! We can only be thankful that we had enough warning to evacuate the whole building!*"

The dinosaurs continued to pummel the first four floors of the Fisher building, angrily lashing out with their powerful jaws, chomping on hard pieces of concrete like it was candy.

Then, the unthinkable happened. The Fisher building began to lurch, slowly at first, and then, without warning, it toppled in upon itself! The entire area was consumed in an explosion of gritty, gray dust. The cloud billowed high into the sky, and the crowd of people in *Burger World* gasped and groaned in horror and disbelief.

In the next instant, the two dinosaurs appeared on the TV screen, emerging from the swirling fog. In my brain, a word came out of nowhere and suddenly lodged itself between my ears. It stuck there, repeating itself over and over.

Unstoppable.

The more I thought about it, the more terror-stricken I became. Would it be possible to actually lure the baby T-Rex—and the two grown T-Rex's—back into the window through time?

Unstoppable. Unstoppable. Unstoppable . . .

Another gasp washed over the crowd, and the camera zoomed in on the dinosaurs. The beasts were running, thundering between buildings and smashing parked cars. They were running at incredible speed, knocking over power lines and destroying everything in their path.

They were headed east—right for our neighborhood!

26

Summer and I both spun at the same time, pushing open the glass doors and running to our bikes. There wasn't a single second to spare.

I rode with one hand on the handlebars and one arm around the bag of steaming cheeseburgers. We pedaled as fast as possible, whizzing down streets, across parking lots, down sidewalks and even over lawns.

My mind swirled. Where was the baby T-Rex?

Was he still in our neighborhood? Had he taken off and gone somewhere else? Would we be able to find him?

My fears were short lived, because as soon as we rounded the corner and turned onto my block, the baby T-Rex found us.

◆◆◆

A movement out of the corner of my left eye caught my attention.

"Nick!" Summer suddenly screamed. *"Look out!!!"*

The baby dinosaur had picked up the scent of the cheeseburgers, and now he was after us!

There was no way I could out-pedal him. He was bounding across a lawn, his eyes on the bag of hot cheeseburgers under my arm. The beast ran through a sprinkler and knocked over a mailbox like it wasn't even there!

"Nick!" Summer shouted again.

I had to do something, but I couldn't pedal any faster.

There was only one thing I could try.

I let go of the handlebars with my right hand and quickly plunged it into the bag tucked under my arm. I grabbed a cheeseburger and launched it over my shoulder, then grabbed the handlebars again, steadying myself as we traveled at breakneck speed. It was pretty tricky, trying to steer with one arm that was holding the bag of cheeseburgers.

To my right, Summer was pedaling madly. She turned to look behind her.

"It worked!" she shouted triumphantly. *"He stopped! He's eating the cheeseburger!"*

Not for long. As soon as I glanced over my shoulder, the baby dinosaur had finished gobbling up the food, and was again in furious pursuit.

A sudden thought came to me. I thought about my first day of school in the fall, and what I would write when my teacher asked us to write an essay about what we did on our summer vacation. Nobody would be able to top *my* story!

I tossed another cheeseburger over my shoulder, then another. Then another. The creature was in the middle of the street, chomping hastily at the cheeseburgers, swallowing paper and all.

"Let's keep going!" I urged frantically. "Let's head for the window through time!"

"But that's miles away from here!" Summer said. "We'll run out of cheeseburgers before we get there!"

"No, we won't," I answered. "We can make it. We won't run out."

At least, I thought, *I hope we won't. We'll have to keep our fingers crossed.*

I threw another cheeseburger over my shoulder, then turned to see how far behind the baby T-Rex was.

But we had a problem I hadn't planned on.

The dinosaur had stopped to gobble up the burger—but right behind him were red and blue flashing lights!

Oh no! It was Mr. Mulroony, the dog catcher! He'd spotted the baby T-Rex!

27

This was a problem. A *serious* problem.

Mr. Mulroony had already stopped his truck and hopped out. He was carrying a long steel pole with a leather slip collar at the end, walking cautiously toward the dinosaur. The baby T-Rex was busy wolfing down a cheeseburger, and paid no attention to the man in the light blue uniform, creeping up behind him.

I skidded to a stop, and when Summer turned

and saw the scene behind me, she stopped, also.

Mr. Mulroony was almost upon the dinosaur—and what's more, he wasn't wearing his glasses!

"Mr. Mulroony!" I shouted, waving a free arm. "Don't! Wait! It's not what you think! It's not a dog!"

Mr. Mulroony didn't pay any attention to me.

In one quick instant he lunged forward, pole extended, and looped the slip collar around the neck of the dinosaur! He actually thought that the baby dinosaur was a *dog!*

This was really dangerous. There was no way that the slip collar would hold the baby T-Rex. The beast could snap the leather snare like a string.

And that's exactly what happened. The dinosaur spun around, lunged sideways, and the leather collar broke in two.

Mr. Mulroony's jaw dropped. I'm sure he wasn't prepared for this. Plus, he didn't have his glasses on, and he didn't realize that he was trying to catch a baby dinosaur!

But now the tables were turned. The dinosaur had turned around to face Mr. Mulroony . . . and I could see right away that we had a serious situation on our hands.

If the baby T-Rex attacked, Mr. Mulroony would be a goner! There was no way he would be able to fight off a charging dinosaur . . . especially a baby T-Rex!

I was seated on my bike, the bag of cheeseburgers still under my arm. I reached into the bag, grabbed a wrapped burger, and let it fly.

Man, I hope my aim is good, I thought, crossing my fingers.

The cheeseburger arched high into the sky. I hoped that it would land close enough to the dinosaur to attract his attention away from Mr. Mulroony.

The cheeseburger sailed overhead, farther, farther—

Oh no! The cheeseburger flew right over top of the dinosaur—and hit Mr. Mulroony square in the face! It fell downward, bounced off of his chest, and hit the ground, coming to a stop at his feet.

Mr. Mulroony took a step back—and just in time, too! The T-Rex had spotted the burger and sprang forward. It picked up the morsel in its jaws and gulped it down.

I had already grabbed another burger, and without hesitating, I let it fly, but the dinosaur was already surging toward his next meal—

Mr. Mulroony!

Mr. Mulroony turned to run, but it was too late. The baby dinosaur was too close, and its powerful jaws snapped and chomped. All of a sudden, Mr. Mulroony let out with a loud, piercing shriek.

"EEEEEAAAAYYYOOOOOWWW!" he cried.

But in the next moment, the cheeseburger that I'd thrown hit the pavement right next to him. The T-Rex saw the tumbling burger and went for it.

The momentary distraction was the break Mr. Mulroony needed. He hobbled to his truck as fast as he could, climbed in, and slammed the door closed. I'm not going to go into details about where Mr. Mulroony had been bitten by the baby dinosaur, but let's just say this: he won't be doing much sitting down for a while.

The dinosaur finished gobbling up the cheeseburger, and once again turned his attention toward Summer and I. He charged toward us, and we were off again, pedaling furiously down the street, the baby T-Rex not far behind.

The plan was actually working well. Summer and I would pedal our bikes and allow the dinosaur to get a few feet behind me. As the dinosaur got closer, Summer would keep an eye on him. On Summer's cue, I would toss another cheeseburger. The dinosaur would chase it, gobble it up, and chase after us again.

We were going to make it. I knew we would. We had enough cheeseburgers to last us until we got to the field where the window through time was.

But there was one big problem that we hadn't planned on.

28

It was something I hadn't even thought about.

Summer and I had turned down a side street, but ahead of us was a busy intersection. There were a lot of cars and trucks whizzing by, and dozens stopped at a traffic light.

That wasn't the problem.

The problem was what was on the other side of the intersection.

A *Burger World* restaurant.

There are a lot of *Burger World* fast-food restaurants around the city, and it wasn't until we were almost at the intersection that I realized we might have a problem.

But it was already too late.

The baby T-Rex had picked up the hot, delicious aromas coming *Burger World!*

I tried to throw the dinosaur off-track by tossing a cheeseburger to him, but he ignored it — and ran right into the intersection of the highway, heading for the restaurant!

The scene was chaotic. Cars screeched to a squealing halt. Horns blared. I could see the incredulous looks from people in stopped vehicles, watching in amazement as the baby dinosaur bounded across the street.

"I can't bear to watch!" Summer exclaimed, throwing her hands up over her face. "He's going to get hit by a car! I just know it!"

There were a couple close calls, but, unbelievably, the dinosaur made it safely to the other side of the intersection. It was a miracle that he hadn't been struck by a car.

But now we had another problem. The people in and around *Burger World* had spotted the dinosaur coming toward them — and they *freaked!* People bolted from the restaurant and ran to their cars, quickly locking their doors. Parents scooped up their children to carry them out of harm's way.

And all the while, the baby dinosaur kept charging . . . up the driveway, through the parking lot . . . *and heading straight for the drive-thru window!*

On the other side of the open window, a woman shrieked in panic as the baby T-Rex raged toward her at full-speed. The woman disappeared for a moment, only to re-appear seconds later, hastily making her way out the side door. Her hands were in the air, and she was screaming like crazy.

The baby dinosaur leapt forward, springing toward the window. There was an enormous crash as the baby T-Rex plunged head-first into the drive-thru window — and got stuck! His body was too big to go through the opening, and the creature was completely off the ground, unable to budge! His clawed legs kicked madly in the air, and his tailed slammed from side to side, smacking into the building.

"Come on!" I yelled to Summer. We took advantage of the confusion in the intersection and pushed our bikes across the street.

"What are we going to do?" Summer asked.
I didn't have the time to answer her. Besides, I wasn't really sure what to do just yet.

We laid our bikes in the grass and ran through the parking lot to the drive through window.

I knew that we had a real problem on our hands, but, I have to admit, the whole scene was pretty darn funny. Seeing the dinosaur's legs and tail flailing in the air was almost comical.

"Let's grab his tail and pull him out!" I said, leaping forward.

"What?!?!?!" Summer exclaimed.

"Grab his tail!" I ordered again. "Quick! Let's grab his tail and pull him out!"

I could tell by the look on Summer's face that she thought I'd lost my mind. Regardless, she followed me up to the drive-thru window where the baby T-Rex was stuck.

The dinosaur's tail swung back and forth, and I reached out with both hands and grabbed the end. His skin was thick and leathery.

Summer reached forward and placed her hands right above mine, and we both began to pull.

"Good . . . *grief!*" I stammered, tugging as hard as I could on the beast's tail. "He's . . . really got . . . himself . . . jammed!"

As we struggled to free the lodged dinosaur, the creature became more and more panicked. I could hear his wails and screeches, and his legs kicked furiously. We had to be careful to watch out for his flailing legs, or else we'd get cut by the T-Rex's razor-sharp claws.

People inside *Burger World* began screaming and hollering, and soon, everyone, including the workers, had left the restaurant. No one wanted to be anywhere close to a raging T-Rex, no matter how big he was.

And yet, here was Summer and I, grasping the tail of the baby dinosaur, pulling with all of our might. People looked at us like we were insane.

We weren't having much luck freeing the beast. Try as we did, the T-Rex remained stuck in the drive-thru window. He kicked and screeched and made an awful fuss.

Suddenly, I heard an explosion from somewhere behind us, down the street. It sounded like a bomb going off.

Then another explosion. And another. Still more. Summer turned, and she let go of the dinosaur's tail.

"Summer!" I shouted. "What are you doing?!?! Help me! We've got to—"

But as I spun to look her in the face, I didn't finish my sentence. Her expression held a look of fear that I had never before seen in her. Summer's face had gone white, the color of fresh cream. I thought she was going to pass out. Still holding onto the tail of the baby T-Rex, I turned to see what she was staring at.

I gasped. I froze. Horror pierced my stomach like a sword.

Two blocks away, smoke was billowing from buildings alongside the highway. Cars had swerved off the road, their horns honking as they tried to get away.

And in the middle of the highway, storming toward us, were the two fully-grown Tyrannosaurus Rex's!

29

Seeing the two Tyrannosaurs coming toward us was worse than a nightmare. Having seen them on TV still hadn't prepared me for what I was now witnessing.

They were monstrous, hideous creatures. Their mouths were open, and, as they walked, they lunged at buildings and cars. Telephone poles split like twigs as the savage beasts thundered past. Electrical wires snapped with an explosion of sparks, but the dinosaurs didn't even notice nor feel any pain from the shower of hot embers.

"They heard the baby T-Rex!" I shouted, putting two and two together. "They must've heard him screeching! Or maybe they picked up his scent!"

There was a sudden crash from behind us. Summer and I both jumped and spun.

The baby T-Rex! He had freed himself! He was only a few feet away from us!

"Come on!" I said to Summer. We raced for our bikes. I scooped up the bag of cheeseburgers.

"Throw one!" Summer shouted as she hopped on her bike.

I reached into the bag, grabbed a burger, and tossed it to the baby T-Rex, who was already charging after us. He saw the cheeseburger on the pavement, and stopped to snare it as it tumbled across the parking lot.

Down the street, the two big dinosaurs had spotted us. They were bearing down, screeching and screaming in anger. Their teeth looked like huge, two-foot daggers protruding from their jaws.

Summer had already started pedaling, and I did the same. The baby dinosaur began to chase us, and I reached into the bag and drew another cheeseburger, letting it fly over my shoulder without looking back.

When I did manage a glance behind us, the sight was like something out of a science fiction movie. We were being chased by a little Tyrannosaurus Rex . . . which was being chased by two HUGE Tyrannosaurs!

I chucked another cheeseburger and glanced back to see the baby gobble it up, still on a dead run. I lobbed the next one high into the air, hopefully buying us some more time.

Time? I thought. I twisted my arm and looked at my watch.

Oh, man! It was five minutes till three! We had only ten minutes to get to the window through time and lead the baby T-Rex back to the Cretaceous period!

"Faster!" I urged Summer. "We have to go faster!" She was riding just to the right of me, and we were both traveling as fast—but we'd have to go faster.

'There's not much time left!" I warned, tossing another cheeseburger over my shoulder. "Or cheeseburgers, for that matter!" I glanced down into the bag. There were only about ten burgers left.

I hoped they would last.

We rode at breakneck speed, right down the

center of the highway. Most of the cars had already spotted the charging dinosaurs and had pulled off to the side of the street. Some people were shouting at us. One old lady rolled down her window and spoke in a loud, angry voice: "Excuse me young man . . . but you're riding your bike without a helmet! That's very dangerous, you know!"

Go figure. I mean, I usually always wear a helmet.

But at this point, I think we were in more danger from the T-Rex's than from anything else!

Behind us, the thundering dinosaurs were getting closer. I could feel the ground tremble and shake with every hulking step they took.

"Over there!" Summer suddenly cried out, pointing.

The field! A wave of relief washed over me. Maybe we would make it in time.

Maybe.

But then again, maybe not.

Because when I turned my head to see how far behind the dinosaurs were, I got the shock of my life. In the next instant, the baby T-Rex lunged forward, kicking the rear wheel of my bike! I closed my eyes and tumbled over the handlebars, head over heels, onto the ground! The bike came crashing down on top of me, and the remaining cheeseburgers went flying.

And when I opened my eyes, the only thing I could see were the two enormous dinosaurs bearing down on me, moving in for the kill.

30

Summer screamed, but I barely heard her. Her shouts were drowned out by the angry snarls from the two Tyrannosaurs. They towered above me, blocking out the sky. Their tongues lashed from side to side, and their jaws chomped up and down in hungry anticipation.

To my left, the baby dinosaur had discovered the spilled bag of cheeseburgers. He was busy, his mouth to the ground, gobbling up the yellow wax-paper hockey pucks.

I threw my bike off me, grabbed three cheeseburgers that were close by, and leapt to me feet. In the same split-instant, I began to run toward the clump of trees on the other side of the field. My heart flailed and banged in my chest, and my breathing was fast and furious.

Ahead of me, Summer shouted words of encouragement.

"You can make it, Nick!" she yelled. "You can make it!"

I managed a quick glance behind me.

The baby dinosaur was occupied with the spilled cheeseburgers, and that had stopped the two bigger dinosaurs from charging after me. They snorted and sniffed at the ground, and their thick, heavy tails swished through the air. The ground trembled beneath their feet.

Still running furiously, I glanced down at my watch.

Three o'clock, on the button! We were almost out of time!

Ahead of me, I could just barely make out the shimmering window. It was a welcome sight, and I pushed myself harder, running faster.

Behind me, one of the dinosaurs let out a loud

snarl, and I turned.

The baby T-Rex had finished eating the cheeseburgers, and now he had his eyes on me! He could smell more cheeseburgers, and now he was racing after me . . . followed closely by the two huge Tyrannosaurs!

Summer had made it to the window through time. She threw down her bike.

"Hurry!" she screamed at me. *"Come on, Nick! Hurry!!"*

I could hear the dinosaurs pounding the ground behind me, and sirens blaring in the distance. The police were on their way, or maybe fire trucks.

Or maybe *both*.

Pushing myself even faster, I stretched my legs as far as they would go. I had to make it to the window. I *had* to.

But there was something else to think about.

If I made it to the window and jumped through with Summer, the dinosaurs wouldn't be able to see me. I'd be millions of years in the past, separated only by the thin window through time.

My only hope was that they would follow me through. What I would do next, I had no idea. But I knew one thing for sure: I had to get the dinosaurs out of Detroit, and back to the Cretaceous period where they belonged.

Back to their home.

Ten steps to go. Nine. Eight—

"Hurry Nick! HURRY!" Summer shrieked.

Seven steps. Six. Five. Four—

"They're right behind you!" she screamed.

Three. Two steps. One.

"Jump!" I shouted, grabbing her hand as I sprang. She grabbed my hand and we both leapt into the air, tucking and rolling as we fell into the window through time.

31

We hit the ground with a thud. Dust and dirt swirled about us. In the distance, the volcano smoldered, spewing black smoke and ashes into the sky. Strange trees and ferns grew all around us.

We were in the Cretaceous era!

I scrambled to my feet and helped Summer off the ground, and we sprinted away from the window. I wanted to be able to get away when the dinosaurs came through.

If the dinosaurs came through.

We waited.

I looked at my watch. It was two minutes after three.

My head was spinning. *What if they don't come through?* I thought. *What if they're stuck in the future for good?!?!*

I looked at my watch. Only two and a half minutes left, and still no dinosaurs.

"Wait here," I said to Summer, and I crept toward the shimmering window. I leaned forward and stuck my head through it . . . and I almost got my head bit off!

The baby dinosaur was right there, just inches away! The two big T-Rex's were just behind him, and when I popped my head through, they freaked. I must've surprised them, since they couldn't see me on the other side of the window. They snarled and growled, lashing out with their tongues, and snapping with their jaws. Again, I caught the whirring of sirens in the distance.

I drew back quickly. In one hand I held a cheeseburger, and I thrust it through the window just for an instant. Then I pulled it back through, slowly and carefully. I hoped to lure the baby dinosaur through the window. If I could get the baby to come through, maybe the other two dinosaurs would follow.

Would it work?

Suddenly, the baby dinosaur's head appeared out of nowhere! He had followed the cheeseburger!

I waved it in front of his nose, and he stretched his neck to grab the snack. I drew it away from him, luring him farther and farther through the window.

When his head and shoulders were completely through, I tossed the cheeseburger to the ground a few feet away.

It worked!

The baby T-Rex lunged through the window, instantly snapping up the tiny cheeseburger. When he was finished, I held out another one, just long enough for him to see it. Then I threw it high into the air, as far as I could, away from me.

The baby T-Rex chased after it like a dog, kicking up dust and dirt as he ran. In seconds he had it in his jaws, gobbling it up.

And right next to me, only a few feet away, a huge snout suddenly appeared.

Then another.

The two dinosaurs were coming back through the window . . . and they were so close I could feel their breath on my skin!

I ran to Summer, and we darted through tall ferns and tucked down into the dense shrubbery, watching.

The two dinosaur heads lurched back and forth, searching.

Then one of the T-Rex's came forward, stepping through the window.

That's it, that's it, I thought. *Just a bit farther. Come on . . . .*

In a sudden surge of explosive power, both Tyrannosaurs lunged through the window! The sound was so loud that both Summer and I cupped our hands over our ears.

It had worked! We had brought the Tyrannosaurs back to the Cretaceous era!

The two dinosaurs spotted the baby dinosaur, and drew closer to him.

Hurray! We'd done it! We had brought the dinosaurs back to where they belonged!

But there was one problem . . . and it was in my hand.

A cheeseburger.

I held the last one in my palm, and the baby T-Rex's keen sense of smell had picked up the scent!

I quickly drew back my arm and let the cheeseburger fly. It sailed up into the air, and the three dinosaurs watched the spinning snack as it hit the ground. The baby dinosaur sprang, gunning for the yellow, wax-paper ball.

I glanced at my watch.

It was four minutes after three! We only had one minute to get back through the window! Otherwise, we'd be stuck here in the Cretaceous era!

"Let's go!" I whispered frantically to Summer.

We sprang from the bushes in a mad dash for the shimmering window.

Forty-five seconds left!

The baby dinosaur was busy chomping down the last cheeseburger, and he wasn't paying much attention. The two big Tyrannosaurs had their backs to us and didn't see us. We continued running for the window.

Thirty seconds. We were going to make it.

Or, so I thought.

Just as we were about to dive through the window, a dark shape sprang toward us from behind a clump of ferns! Summer and I skidded to a stop.

"Oh no!" Summer screamed. "What's that?!"

I couldn't believe what I was seeing! But, then again, I couldn't believe what had happened this past week, either.

The beast that threatened us stormed closer,

and I knew what it was.

A Megaraptor! He was right in front of the window through time, blocking our only way back to our time period!

And if you know anything about a Megaraptor, you would know that we were about to be torn to shreds.

32

A Megaraptor is a vicious, bird-like dinosaur. This one was about twenty feet long, and had a curved, flexible neck and a big head, and rows of sharp, serrated teeth capable of ripping its prey into a million pieces.

And he had his eyes on *us!*

Summer and I took a few quick steps back. There was no escape, and the Megaraptor was blocking our flight to the window through time!

Suddenly, there was a loud screech from behind us. The startling noise drew the attention of the Megaraptor, and it turned.

Without warning, one of the Tyrannosaurs attacked! It charged toward the Megaraptor, and suddenly the two dinosaurs were in a terrible battle to the finish!

I looked at my watch. We only had fifteen seconds!

"Nick!" Summer screamed, shouting above the noise of the fighting dinosaurs. "Look!"

The window through time was fading! The gray fuzziness was dissipating right before our eyes.

"We have to go!" I shouted urgently. *"Now!"* I grabbed Summer's hand and we bounded toward the window, only a few feet from the battling dinosaurs. They were screeching and lunging at each other, creating a terrible noise.

Only five seconds left!

"Dive!" I shouted at the top of my lungs. *"Dive through the window!"*

Summer and I leapt into the air at the very last moment.

Suddenly, the thundering of the dinosaurs was replaced by the wailing of sirens. I heard voices barking orders, car doors slamming in the distance, and helicopters in the air.

I hit the ground first, followed immediately by Summer. I hastily snapped to my feet, and glanced back just in time to see the shimmering window fade from a misty gray to a dusty, white film. It wavered for a moment, and in the next moment, it was gone.

The window through time had closed for another fifty years.

Summer stood up and dusted herself off.

"Man," she said shakily. "I can't believe that just happened. I just *can't* believe it happened."

"Believe it," I assured her, shaking my head. "Believe it."

The sirens grew louder, and suddenly, a police car came into view on the other side of the field. Then another, and then a fire truck flew past.

"Come on," I said. "Let's go home."

That night as Mom, Dad, and I sat around the dinner table, all we talked about were the dinosaurs. Of course, I didn't say a thing about what I knew about the whole thing. There is no way Mom or Dad would have believed me, anyway.

The news reports said that the Tyrannosaurs

had simply seemed to vanish into thin air, and they were nowhere to be found. Experts from around the world were being flown in to investigate. Television psychics were offering their opinions, but I could tell they were just making stuff up to get attention.

Remarkably, and much to my relief, not one person in Detroit or the surrounding cities had been seriously hurt. A lot of buildings had been destroyed, and I had lost my bicycle. It had been crushed by one of the dinosaurs as it chased us through the field.

Which was no great loss, when you consider all of the other problems we could have had!

I went to bed that night feeling like a huge weight had been lifted from my shoulders.

But when I woke up the next morning, I got the shock of my life.

I had just finished a bowl of cereal and turned the television on. There, on the screen before me, were the two dinosaurs! The reporter was talking about how the dinosaurs were ravaging the city! Somehow—some way—the Tyrannosaurs had returned!

I stood for a moment, my mouth gaping open. Terror flooded my entire body. I ran to the phone and called Summer.

The phone rang and rang. Finally, Summer's voice cracked over the phone. I could tell I had woke her up.

"Hello?" she said groggily.

"Summer!" I shouted. "They're back! The dinosaurs somehow came back through time!"

"What?!?!" she screeched in my ear. *"How?!?! When?!?!"*

"Turn your TV on! You'll see!"

I heard her put the phone down. She was gone for what seemed like a long time. In the other room of my house, I could hear the television news reporters talking about the dinosaurs.

Finally, I heard her pick up the phone.

"Don't be ridiculous," she said. "All they're doing is replaying some of the footage from yesterday! I'm going back to bed!"

There was an abrupt click on the other end of the phone. Summer was gone.

I hung the receiver up and dashed into the living room.

She was right. The TV station was just replaying the footage from the day before. I shook my head and heaved a huge sigh of relief.

At the beginning of the school year, the first day was just as I suspected. In my English class, we were all instructed to write a two-page paper about what we did on our summer vacation.

I decided *not* to mention anything about

dinosaurs or windows through time. Instead, I wrote about a fishing trip that I took with my dad.

When we were finished, the teacher called on a few students to read their paper to the class. I wasn't chosen, and I was glad.

But there was a new kid in class who was, and when he read his story, everyone laughed at him! He said that a friend of his in Saginaw had battled an invasion of *spiders!*

Everyone laughed and laughed — except me. Somehow, I had a feeling he was telling the truth.

After he was finished, everybody just snickered and cracked jokes. I felt bad for him. The teacher just smiled, said that he'd done a nice job, and called on another student.

Later that day, in the lunchroom, I went up to the new kid and introduced myself. I asked him about his spider story.

"It's not my story," he explained. "It happened to my friend, Leah Warner. In Saginaw."

I knew where Saginaw was. I'd been there a couple of times, and Dad and I went fishing once in the Saginaw River. I caught a huge bass on that trip.

"What happened?" I asked him. "Can you tell me about it?"

"Better," he answered. He pushed aside his

sandwich and opened up his backpack. "Leah wrote everything down in a journal. Here it is. You can read it, but you have to give it back when you're done, because I need to return it to her. But I have to warn you . . . what she went through was awful. It was a nightmare. And it's *true.*"

That night, after I finished dinner, I went to my bedroom and opened up Leah Warner's journal.

And I started to read.

NEXT IN THE 'MICHIGAN CHILLERS SERIES:

#9: SINISTER SPIDERS OF SAGINAW

TURN THE PAGE FOR A FEW CREEPY CHAPTERS!

There were two things that happened that day, and both should have given me a clue as to what was about to come. The first thing happened when I was doing my homework.

It was five-thirty in the morning. I like getting up early to work on my homework. It's really quiet, and my older brother isn't awake to bug me. I was at the dining table, working on my math. Mom had just woke up, and she came into the kitchen.

"My goodness, Leah," she said, yawning as she

strode into the room. "How long have you been up?"

"Not long," I replied, putting my pencil down. "I just need to go over the answers on my homework."

Leah is my name. Leah Warner. I'm thirteen, and I live in Saginaw. It's a pretty cool city, and there's a lot of history here. Saginaw began in 1816 as a fur-trading post. The name 'Saginaw', like a lot of Michigan cities, is actually a Native American name. 'O-Sag-A-Nong' means 'land of the Sauks'. That's where the word 'Saginaw' comes from.

But after what was about to happen, you might call Saginaw the 'land of the spiders.'

I *hate* spiders. I absolutely *hate* them. I mean, I know that they serve their purpose and everything by eating bugs and stuff, but spiders are just so . . . *gross.* They're fine if they leave me alone, but if I see one in the house, he's history.

Like the one that was climbing on my leg that morning.

Mom had just left the kitchen, and I returned to my homework. I had my nose in a book, and was double-checking the answers on my math paper. We were going to have a quiz today. Ug.

I felt a light tickling on my ankle, and I looked down.

It was a spider. Not a big one, mind you—but that didn't matter. It was a *spider*, and it was crawling on *me*. I about jumped out of my skin!

"Yaaaa!" I shrieked, dropping my pencil and smacking my leg with the palm of my hand. The awful bugger crushed under my hard slap, and, as I wiped him away, the tiny creature balled up and fell to the floor, dead.

"Eewww," I moaned, staring down at the lifeless spider on the floor.

Our dog, Grumpy, heard me, and waddled into the room. Grumpy is a brown cocker spaniel. If you wake him up from a sleep, he lays on the ground and growls at you. Oh, he'd never bite you. He's just grumpy—and that's how he got his name. My older brother, Scott, found him as a puppy. We've had Grumpy for almost five years.

Grumpy walked over to me, sniffed the floor—and ate the dead spider!

"Eeeww!! Grumpy!" I said, wincing. "That's sick!" Grumpy wagged his tail, turned around, and bounded happily away.

Silly dog. I can't believe he would actually eat a spider!

Of course, a lot of things were about to happen that I wouldn't believe. Things that I wouldn't have imagined in a million years.

Later that day, after school, I rode the bus home and sprinted to the front door of our house. We live on Hamilton Street, and our house is only a mile from my school. Sometimes I ride my bike. Scott almost always rides his bike, except in the winter, so he usually makes it home before I do. The bus ride can be kind of long.

I burst through the door, my backpack in hand — and froze in horror.

There, on the living room floor, was a tarantula.

2

I froze in complete horror. The spider was huge, ugly, and *nasty*. It was the biggest spider I've ever seen. It was black and brown and looked like it had fur all over its body. Two big, black eyes stared menacingly back at me. It was the most hideous, horrible creature I'd ever seen in my life.

Grumpy was there, his hackles raised and teeth bared. He was only a few feet away from the spider. He snarled and snapped, but he kept his distance from the enormous creature on the carpet.

My backpack fell to the floor, and my mouth opened wide. I tried to scream, but no sound would come out. My whole body shook.

Suddenly, the spider *moved!* One of his legs raised up slowly, and the spider inched toward me.

This was a nightmare! Worse . . . it was really happening! Oh, how I *wished* it was a nightmare. Then I could wake up!

But this wasn't any dream at all. There was a spider—a *huge* one—not five feet away from me!

Grumpy continued to snarl and bark, but he kept his distance. This was one spider he was *not* going to eat!

I stood there, unable to move, when I suddenly heard snickering coming from the hall. I saw a shadow move, then I heard more giggling.

Suddenly, Scott came into the living room wearing a mischievous grin. He walked right over to the spider . . . and picked it up!

"Like my pet?" he said, placing the spider in his palm.

Wait a minute, I thought. *There's something kind of strange about that spider . . . .*

Bravely, I took a step forward, my eyes focused on the ugly, dark creature in Scott's hand.

"Check it out," he urged. "But be careful. He

might bite you."

Closer . . . .

"You goofball!" I suddenly cried. "That's not a *real* spider!"

And it wasn't! Now that I had a closer look, I could see that the spider wasn't real, after all. It was fake! A very *good* fake, at that. It really looked like an *actual* spider!

"Cool, huh?" he said, still wearing a cat-like grin. "I bought it at the gag-gift store. It was on sale." He flipped it over in his hand, pointing to an on/off switch on the spider's belly. He clicked the switch off. "See? It's battery-operated."

"Yeah, real cool," I snapped. I punched him in the shoulder so hard that he dropped the spider.

"Ouch!" he exclaimed. "That hurt!" He bent over to pick up the spider.

"You deserved it!" I said angrily, storming past him. My anger boiled, and I stomped across the living room to my bedroom, slamming the door closed behind me.

Brothers, I thought, shaking my head. *They should be illegal. Brothers should be against the law.*

But there was one thing that made me happy. Today was Thursday . . . and Scott would be leaving for band camp tomorrow morning. He'd be gone for two whole days! Hurray! Not only that, it was a 'teacher in-service' day, which meant we wouldn't have any school Friday! I couldn't wait. Two whole days of peace and quiet. No Scott, no stupid pranks. Just me and Mom and Dad and Grumpy.

Peace and quiet.

Of course, peace and quiet was the last thing that I would have. I certainly didn't know it then, but soon, I would encounter spiders — real spiders — that were a hundred times bigger than the fake tarantula Scott had scared me with.

3

Friday morning, I slept in. The house was quiet until Scott woke up. He began racing around the house, looking for this and that, trying to pack all of his clothes at the last minute. As for me, I was snuggled in bed doing simple math in my head. I was counting the seconds until Scott would leave for band camp.

After he left, I made some toast and a cup of hot chocolate. The warm liquid tasted sweet and good. I was feeling better already. Scott had only been gone five minutes, and I was already more relaxed. No pranks, no stupid jokes for two whole days. No dorky brother hanging around the house, bugging me.

Just Mom, Dad, Grumpy and myself.

Cool. I was in such a good mood that morning that I went for a walk in the park, just by myself, enjoying the day, taking my time, breathing in the fresh spring air.

■■■

When I returned, Mom and Dad had already left for work, so I found the key to let myself in. We have a house key that we keep under a rock next to the porch, but don't tell anyone.

I found the key, unlocked the door, and let myself in—and right away, I knew something was wrong. I could just *feel* it.

What was it?

I stopped in the doorway, looking around the living room. The house was silent, which wouldn't be unusual. But it was *too* silent.

What was it?

And suddenly, I knew.

Grumpy. He always greets me at the door. He greets *everyone* at the door.

But not today.

"Grumpy?" I said loudly, stepping into the living room. I expected him to come running, but he didn't. The house was quiet.

"Grumpy?" I called again, raising my voice even louder.

No dog. This was really weird.

I walked into the kitchen, and found a yellow sticky-note on the fridge. It read:

Leah

Your father and I will both be working late tonight . . . should be home around eight. Make yourself a sandwich for lunch. For dinner, there's some leftover lasagna in the refrigerator – just nuke it for a few minutes. Oh . . . I let Grumpy outside. Can you let him in when you get back from your walk? Call me at the office if you need anything. Love ya lots!

–Mom

Okay—so Mom and Dad weren't going to be home for a while.

I walked to the sliding glass door to let Grumpy in. Our back yard has a fence that goes all the way around it. Grumpy can run and play in our yard without wandering off.

But Grumpy was nowhere to be found! He wasn't in the back yard.

"Grumpy!" I shouted. "Come here, boy!"

No Grumpy. But as I looked around the yard, I realized what had happened.

Grumpy likes to dig holes. And today, he'd dug a hole right under the fence! Grumpy had ran away!

Shoot, I thought. Once in a while, Grumpy gets out of the yard and wanders the neighborhood. He usually doesn't go too far, but we have to go look for him.

Which is what I would have to do. I couldn't bear the thought of Grumpy wandering into a road or a highway. I had to find him fast.

But I wasn't going to search for him alone. I called up Angela Meyer and Conner Karpinski, two of my best friends. Both live only a few houses away. They rushed over to help me find Grumpy.

"Where did you see him last?" Conner said, placing his hands on his hips and looking around the yard. Conner is twelve, but he's taller than I am. Actually, he's the tallest kid in our grade.

"Well, I haven't seen him since this morning,"

I replied. "When I got home from a walk, he was gone. He'd dug a hole under the fence and crawled under it."

"He can't be far," Angela offered hopefully. She sounded positive and optimistic. That's one of the things I like about Angela: she always looks on the bright side of things. I've known Angela since the second grade. Her family came to the United States from a small town in South Africa. She tells me fascinating stories about growing up when she was really young.

We decided that, to find Grumpy quickly, we'd have to split up. I would go north and search a few blocks over, while Conner would go across the street and search some of the alleys and back streets

Angela said she would go down to the old drainage ditch where there are lots of trees. It's kind of a swampy area, and I've never hung around there much. Nobody does. There are a lot of weird stories about the drainage ditch . . . crazy, bizarre stories. I've always ignored them.

But I've stayed away, just in case.

We searched and searched for nearly an hour without any luck. Conner and I finally met up again at our house. We waited for Angela.

And we waited.

But Angela never came back. She never returned, so we decided to go look for her . . . at the old drainage ditch.

And what we were about to encounter was the scariest thing that had ever happened to me in my entire life.

4

The drainage ditch isn't far from where we live. Conner and I walked down the sidewalk, completely unaware of the terrible circumstances that were about to befall us.

"Where does Grumpy like to go when he runs off?" Conner asked.

"All over the place," I answered, rolling my eyes. "Grumpy just likes cruising around and checking things out."

We kept our eyes peeled as we walked, looking

for signs of the dog. Once, I spotted a movement in a yard, but it was someone else's dog.

And then we came to the old drainage ditch.

We should have know that something was wrong, right off the bat. The trees and brush just seemed to be cold and lifeless. The whole area was dark and strange. Which was kind of odd, because the day was sunny and warm.

I cupped my hands around my mouth. "Angela!" I shouted into the forest. "Angela?!?!? Are you around here?!?!?"

No answer.

Conner and I jumped over the drainage ditch. It's about three feet wide, and, three feet deep. When it rains, the ditch fills up with water and runs off. Today there wasn't much water in the ditch at all.

"Angela?!?!?" I called out again. "Where are you?"

As we approached the trees, we were enveloped by shade. Still, I couldn't help feeling like we were walking into some strange world or something. It was a spooky feeling.

"Have you ever been in here?" I asked Conner, looking around.

He shook his head. "Nope," he replied. "I can think of better places to hang out."

198

"Me too," I said, staring up at an old, dead oak tree. "But, I imagine, Grumpy would probably like playing around in the woods."

"He's probably rolling around in the mud as we speak," Conner said, smiling.

"Oh, don't say that," I replied. "Then I'll have to give him a bath before Mom and Dad come home. I'll have to—"

Conner suddenly grasped my arm.

"Shhhhhh," he whispered.

We stopped walking, and listened. In the distance, I could hear the rush of cars on the highway. A horn honked a long ways off, and an airplane buzzed somewhere high overhead.

"What is it?" I asked quietly.

Conner paused a moment, then answered. "Well," he said, a bit louder, "I guess it was nothing. I just though that I heard something, that's all. Something moving. It must have been my imagination."

The problem was, it *wasn't* his imagination, as we were about to find out.

■■■

The wooded area around the drainage ditch

isn't very big. Sure, there are quite a few trees and shrubs in the small two-acre tract, but there really isn't any way you could get lost. In two minutes, you could walk through the woods and be back in the subdivision.

We walked along a dense path. I was becoming more and more worried by the minute. I was worried about Grumpy, but now, I was more worried about Angela. It wasn't like her to just disappear like that.

"Do you think she went home?" Conner considered. "She doesn't seem to be anywhere around here." He stopped walking, and stood next to a big, dead stump. Blades of sunlight sliced through the trees, and I looked around. There wasn't any sign of Grumpy or Angela. Or anyone else, for that matter. No footprints, no sounds, nothing.

"No," I responded to Conner's question. "She would have told us. She wouldn't have gone home without letting us know."

Suddenly, a twig snapped on the other side of the stump. Conner jumped, and I did, too. Then I laughed.

"Gosh, we're both a bit jumpy in these woods," I said.

But Conner didn't hear a single word I said.

He took several quick steps backward, and I noticed that he was shaking.

"Conner?" I said. "Conner . . . what's wrong?"

He was really trembling now, and he was trying to speak—but no sound came from his lips. He raised his hand to point, and I could see his arm shaking badly.

"Conner?!?!?" I said again. I was worried. There was something wrong with him.

I looked at the stump he was pointing at, and a surge of horror hit me like a truck. My heart stopped. My skin crawled. My hair stood on end.

The 'stump' that Conner was pointing at was not a stump at all—*it was a spider!*

It was a living, moving, live spider, the size of a picnic table. It was black, and had long, sinewy legs. Glaring, shiny eyes, the size of bowling balls, were focused on Conner and I. Two dagger-like fangs protruded from the spider's mouth.

And it *moved!* It began to move, slowly, cautiously, one leg at a time—toward us!!

I've seen science fiction movies before, and I've seen some pretty scary, gross movies, too.

But this was no movie, and the terror I felt now was ten times worse than any movie I've ever seen. A *thousand* times worse.

"Don't budge a muscle," Conner managed to whisper. His lips barely moved. "Maybe he can't see us."

I didn't tell Conner, but I couldn't have moved if I tried! I was too horrified by what I was seeing. It couldn't be real. Somehow, this had to be someone's idea of a joke. Probably my brother, Scott.

But then again, I knew this was no joke. I knew that we were looking at a real, honest-to-goodness spider. How it was possible, I didn't know. I didn't know what kind it was, and I didn't care. All I knew was that we were in *big* trouble.

Looking back, I don't think it would have mattered if we'd tried to run. Spiders are incredibly fast, as we were about to find out.

The huge, black creature seemed to be stalking us, creeping slowly forward, coming closer and closer. Conner was in the creature's path. I had managed to back up a few more feet down the trail, away from the monstrous spider.

"Conner!" I said anxiously. "We have to get away! We have to run!"

The spider took another step toward Conner. Conner suddenly began to turn to run—but it was too late.

All at once, a sticky, stringy substance shot through the air like lightning, striking Conner on the shoulder. When he tried to wipe it away, his hand stuck to it.

"Hey!" he shouted. "What's—"

He didn't have time to finish his words. In the

blink of an eye he was covered with a white, sticky, stringy web. *The spider was wrapping him up!*

"Leah!" he panicked, as strands of web began to cover his mouth and face. "Leah! Help me! *HELP ME!!*"

In a flash, the spider was upon him. The hideous creature grasped Conner with three of its claw-like legs, spinning him around, wrapping him in silky-white webbing. There was nothing I could do to help my friend. It was a horrible, gut-wrenching feeling, knowing that I couldn't help Conner.

The only thing I could do was run. I could run, and try and get help. I would run all the way to the police station if I had to. Maybe it wouldn't be too late to save Conner.

Maybe.

But then again, maybe it was . . . because when I turned to flee down the path, I was face-to-face with another spider!

This one was even bigger than the one that had attacked Conner! It was brown and hairy with six eyes. Legs as thick as telephone poles raised and lowered as the spider walked toward me. Branches snapped and cracked as the gargantuan creature approached.

And then, I too, was hit by the strange, silky

webbing. I tried to wipe it away, but my hand stuck to it! More of the gooey material hit me, and I tried swiping it off with my other hand. It stuck, too!

I let out a scream. It was loud, long, and shrill. I screamed with everything I had, hoping that someone would hear.

The spider lunged, and, in an instant, was upon me. Strong legs picked me up in the air, and at once I was spinning, tossed round and round. The white stringy web bound my legs, my hands and arms. It covered my eyes, my nose, my face. The only thing I could see were the shiny strands of web that were covering my eyes. I couldn't move an inch.

Then, everything began to go dark. Everything suddenly went black, and I passed out.

But the worst was yet to come.

DINOSAURS DESTROY DETROIT WORD SEARCH!

```
Y J D N I V E A U N I Y O A L T W D K S
D P O U U Z C I C M T V S T D H X Y U A
N B Q C A K Q K W W I B M D J L T H O W
Y M U Z C G Y M R D S L S U S M Y D R G
E N B S V K M B H R G R T D U S E R W L
T J O U C A M N R Y N D G L L A R I J V
E R W O D H C O B C I C I A T L N W I C
C M I E R D E A Q R D C V N A D N H C Q
B O Z C I L L E M P L A J E O T O L S J
J K U A E G U R S S I Y I W C S S R C Y
X Z D T U R Y M O E U Z T B L I A C N G
N M Q E W D A F R W B H B X A N U U C C
I G J R F I P T Q M R U D S Z P R R R I
O B H C B P O G O O E E R X T B U R F S
Q K A Z V L Y C U P H K G G Z F S Z P S
X Q T T I Z B G Q H S H Q R E G R R U A
K C I N O Y H A W F I A K X U R E W V R
V X O T V T E Z B F F J A P Q B X A P U
H H R R I E N T K Y O D U C T C N Q C J
M W T M E G A R A P T O R C G S R G T P
N X E I C M E R O Z J R R O W W J V U L
G M D T A D M Y K Q D H E A H G Q L R C
I Q E B E Y N U G W E K N X T Y M Z J H
L U F A G A D R S P L C C L P G Y D T K
```

Tyrannosaurus Rex
Jurassic
Dinosaurs
Nick
Summer
Detroit
Queztzalcoatlus
Triceratops

Mr. Mulroony
Baby T-Rex
Cheeseburger
Cretaceous
Fisher Building
Burger World
Megaraptor
Window Through Time

WORD SCRAMBLE!

REBGRU RODLW — Burger World

OAIURNSD — DINOSAUR

STRRIOETCPA — _ _ _ _ _ _ _ _ _ _

CNKI — Nick

ABXY R TEB — BABY T Rex

MRGPOREATA — _ _ _ _ _ _ _ _ _

HSFRIE DBGNULII — _ _ _ _ _ _ _ _ _ _ _ _

MUSEMR — _ _ _ _ _ _

TRTEOID — Detroit

RL OMRUYOMN — Mr MULROONY

OYRNARNATSU — TYRANOSAURUS

AUSIJCSR — JURASSIC

USREETCAOE — _ _ _ _ _ _ _ _ _ _

208

GHOST IN THE GRAVEYARD

GHOST IN THE GRAVEYARD

is the first compilation of short stories from Michigan author Johnathan Rand! Stories include 'Bigfoot Runs Amok', 'The Hidden Door', 'Ghost in the Graveyard', and MORE!

"These stories are TOO COOL!" - Justin G., age 11, Chicago, IL

"GREAT STORIES! If you like the 'Chillers' series, you'll love 'GHOST IN THE GRAVEYARD'! - Amanda K., age 9, Livonia, MI

'GHOST IN THE GRAVEYARD' is awesome! I can't wait for more books like this one!" - Tyler S., age 13, Denver, CO.

"All of my students LOVE 'GHOST IN THE GRAVEYARD'!"
- Bryan Randle, teacher, Gladwin, MI

Find out more at www.ghostinthegraveyard.net

Join Johnathan Rand as he travels! Check out *www.michiganchillers.com* for Mr. Rand's on-line journal, featuring pictures and stories during his journeys! It's like traveling with him yourself! You'll get the inside scoop on when and where he'll be, and what projects he's working on right now!

Visit www.michiganchillers.com!

About the cover art: This unique cover was designed and created by Michigan artists Darrin Brege and Mark Thompson.

Darrin Brege works as an animator by day, and is now applying his talents on the internet, creating various web sites and flash animations. He attended animation school in southern California in the early nineties, and over the years has created original characters and animations for Warner Bros (Space Jam), for Hasbro (Tonka Joe Multimedia line), Universal Pictures (Bullwinkle and Fractured Fairy Tales CD Roms), and Disney. Besides art, he and his wife Karen are improv performers featured weekly at Mark Ridley's Comedy Castle over the last six years. Improvisational comedy has provided the groundwork for a successful voice over career as well. Darrin has dozens of characters and impersonations in his portfolio and, most recently, provided Columbia Tri-Star pictures with a Nathan Lane 'sound alike' for Stuart Little. Speaking of little, Darrin and Karen also have a little son named Mick.

Mark Thompson, also known as THE ICEMAN, has been in the illustration field for over 20 years, working for everyone from the Detroit Tigers, Ameritech, as well as auto companies and toy companies such as Hasbro and Mattel. Mark's main interests are in science fiction and fantasy art. He works from his studio in a log home in the woods of Hamburg, Michigan. Mark is married with 2 children, and he is also a big-time horror fan and comic collector!

Announcing a BRAND NEW SERIES from best-selling author Johanthan Rand!

AMERICAN CHILLERS

#1: The Michigan Mega-Monsters

Now available!

Visit

www.americanchillers.com!

About the author

Much has changed for Johnathan Rand and his wife since the introduction of the 'Michigan Chillers' series in March of 2000. The books have become one of the best-selling series in the Midwest, now with over 250,000 copies in print. In addition to the 'Michigan Chillers' series, Rand is also the author of **'Ghost in the Graveyard'** a collection of thrilling short stories featuring *The Adventure Club.* (And don't forget to check out www.ghostinthegraveyard.com and read an entire story for *FREE!*) When they are not traveling to schools and book signings, Mr. Rand and his wife live in a small town in northern lower Michigan, with their two dogs, Abby and Salty. He still writes all of his books in the wee hours of the morning, and still submits all manuscripts by mail. He is currently working on his newest series, entitled **'American Chillers'**.